ROCKFORD PUBLIC LIBRARY

Rockford, Illinois

www.rockfordpubliclibrary.org

815-965-9511

THE
BIG TIME

HARPER

An Imprint of HarperCollinsPublishers

BIG ME

A FOOTBALL GENIUS NOVEL

TIM GREEN

ALSO BY TIM GREEN

FOOTBALL GENIUS NOVELS

Football Genius

Football Hero

Football Champ

The Big Time

BASEBALL GREAT NOVELS

Baseball Great

Rivals

Best of the Best

The Big Time: A Football Genius Novel

Copyright © 2010 by Tim Green

All rights reserved. Printed in the United States of America.

No part of this book may be used or reproduced in any manner whatsoever without written permission except in the case of brief quotations embodied in critical articles and reviews. For information address HarperCollins Children's Books, a division of HarperCollins Publishers, 10 East 53rd Street, New York, NY 10022.

www.harpercollinschildrens.com

Library of Congress Cataloging-in-Publication Data is available.

ISBN 978-0-06-168619-1 (trade bdg.)

ISBN 978-0-06-168620-7 (lib. bdg.)

Typography by Joel Tippie

10 11 12 13 14   LP/RRDH   10 9 8 7 6 5 4 3 2 1

❖

First Edition

For my brother, Kenny, because you're big time

CHAPTER ONE

ALL HIS LIFE, TROY dreamed of meeting the father he never knew. Never once did he imagine it would turn into a nightmare. Still, the rage oozing from his mother's voice when she saw his father's face wasn't a complete surprise. But when her hateful glare scorched Troy, too? That was a shocker.

She acted as if Troy had invited the man to show up on Seth Halloway's front steps when, in fact, the appearance of his missing father shook Troy to the core.

"We don't want you here," Troy's mom said.

Seth, the Falcons' star linebacker, appeared behind her and stepped onto the front porch of his stone mansion as if to protect Troy and his friends, Tate and Nathan, from the intruder. Noise from the party by

1

the pool out back filtered up over the slate roof and into the night sky. The entire Duluth Tigers football team—which Seth had coached as a favor to Troy—and the players' parents were celebrating the team's victory in the Georgia Junior League Football State Championship.

"Can I help you?" Seth asked, the cords in his muscular neck now dancing in the porch light.

Troy's father stood an inch or two over six feet—as tall as Seth—with a handsome face worn from weather and worry. He laughed a soft, friendly laugh, and he stuck out a big hand with a slim gold watch on his wrist.

"I'm Drew Edinger; I'm staying with a client who lives a few streets away," Troy's dad said, extending his hand even farther until Seth had no choice but to shake it. "I know who you are. I admire the way you play."

"I said we don't want you here," Troy's mom said, crossing her arms and jutting out her jaw.

"I'm the boy's father."

"You're not his father," Troy's mom said.

Drew looked at Troy, gave him a sly wink, and said, "You're saying he belongs to someone else?"

CHAPTER TWO

"HE BELONGS TO *ME*," Troy's mom said, "the one who changed his diapers and bathed him and cooked for him and helped him with his homework and took care of him when he was sick. Just because he's got half your genes doesn't make you a father."

Drew turned his attention back to her, shook his head, and said, "You haven't changed a bit, have you, Tessa? Still beautiful. Still full of vinegar."

Troy's mom pointed a finger toward the street. "Go."

"You think this boy doesn't deserve to know his father?" Drew asked, his heavy eyebrows settling in on his brow. "At least a little bit? What do you think, Troy?"

Troy felt his mouth sag open, but no words spilled

out. He looked at Tate. She had good sense, better than he and Nathan. Her big brown eyes widened, but she only shrugged her shoulders in confusion.

"You're twelve years too late, Drew," Troy's mom said. "Don't make us call the police."

"Police?" Drew said, raising his eyebrows.

"Tessa," Seth said, speaking quietly. "Let's not go crazy here."

"I didn't even know Troy existed until I saw you and him on TV with Larry King," Drew said, his hands splayed open, his voice nearly begging. "I knew then. He looks just like me."

"I *told* you," Troy's mom said.

"You never told me *anything*," Drew said. "We fought about getting married and having kids, something you wanted and I didn't. Back then, with my injury and hoping I could make a comeback, my whole life was a mess. I never knew we had a *son*. You think I wouldn't have seen him all this time? You think I wouldn't have helped pay for things? I've done well, Tessa, even without football."

"I'm not going back in time to do this all over again," Troy's mom said. "I've moved on. We're fine."

"But you never told me," Drew said. "He deserves to know the truth, Tessa. I can't imagine what he must think."

"He thinks what he thinks," Troy's mom said.

"You need to tell him," Drew said.

Troy felt dizzy. "Mom?"

"He knew," she said, raising her voice and stabbing her finger at Drew. "Maybe I didn't throw myself at his feet and beg him to stay, but he *knew*."

"In law school they teach you to ask if innocence is *possible*," Drew said.

"I'm not a lawyer," she said.

"I am," he said, winking quickly at Troy again. "It's called presumption of innocence. It's what separates us from Attila the Hun. Think about it. Isn't it possible— given what I was going through at the time—that I didn't put two and two together?"

"You were a math major," she said. "Adding two and two was something you shouldn't have missed."

"Maybe I shouldn't have," Drew said, nodding. "Okay, I agree; but I'm asking you if it's *possible* that I did. Isn't it? Couldn't me not being around for Troy all this time be a big mistake?"

Troy looked at his mom. Her lower lip disappeared beneath her top teeth as she studied Drew Edinger.

"Tessa, if you tell me no," Drew said, pointing down the stone path toward the driveway and the Porsche convertible in which he'd pulled up, "then I'll walk away, go back to Chicago, and neither of you will ever see me again."

Troy held his breath.

CHAPTER THREE

TROY'S MOM'S GLARE FADED. She hung her head and quietly said, "You were always clever, Drew. I bet you're some lawyer."

"That means you agree," Troy's father said, pushing back the flaps of his leather blazer so he could plant his hands on the waist of his jeans.

"No," she said, shaking her head so that the sheets of her long brown hair fell in a curtain about her face. She looked up with burning eyes. "I won't agree. I'd still like you to leave now. We're having a celebration, and you weren't invited. You're not part of my life, and you're not part of Troy's. You missed your chance. Go."

Drew's face fell. He dropped his hands and shifted his cowboy boots so that they scuffed the grit on the stone stoop. "You can't just—"

6

Seth stepped forward and held his hand up like a traffic cop, almost touching Drew's chest. "No. She asked you to leave, so you need to do that."

Troy saw the flicker of anger in his father's eyes. His jaws were working side to side, and his hands curled into fists.

Troy stood paralyzed by it all—unable to move, unable to think, barely able to breathe.

"Don't do this," Seth said, quiet and almost friendly.

Then the fire went out. Troy's father cast a sad, almost desperate look at Troy before he turned and retreated down the stone walkway. The orange Porsche's lights blazed and the engine revved, then the car shot out backward into the road. The tires yelped, and the Porsche surged up the street to be swallowed by the night.

Troy descended the steps, moving in the car's direction until he stood alone on the edge of the light where it met the shadows of the front lawn's towering trees.

"Dad?" he said.

CHAPTER FOUR

"MY GOD," TROY'S MOM said under her breath.

Troy looked up at her as she turned and disappeared into Seth's house before reappearing to say "Troy, get your things. You've got a big day tomorrow."

Troy looked at his friends. Seth frowned and followed Troy's mother back inside. Nathan scowled in confusion. Tate tilted her head to one side, looking into Troy's eyes as if she could read his feelings. Her eyes glistened with sadness and concern.

Tate descended the steps and touched his arm. Speaking quietly, she asked, "Troy, are you okay?"

"I—I don't know," he said, taking a deep breath and letting it go. Troy felt suddenly tired and sore. The finger he'd dislocated during the championship game throbbed, and the thrill of winning sputtered under the storm of feelings about his father.

His mom reappeared on the front steps with her purse. Seth followed, and she kissed him good-bye, all business.

"Okay, Troy," she said, coming down the steps and past him on the walkway toward where her pale green VW bug waited in the driveway.

Troy wanted to go back to the party and reclaim the joy of the victory celebration. He opened his mouth to protest going home. His mom stopped where the stone walk met the driveway and turned as if she sensed his resistance. The look she gave him changed his mind. He said good night and thanked Seth for coaching the team to victory.

"Don't worry," Tate said, "we're going home now, too."

Troy hustled after his mom, his face hot with shame from some unknown source.

They rode in silence, exiting the Cotton Wood Country Club through massive gates and essentially circling a huge block of county highways to their own home down a winding dirt road. Their house, a single-story saltbox not much bigger than a cabin, sat amid a cluster of pines just the other side of the train tracks and a ten-foot concrete wall surrounding the exclusive development where Seth lived. When they pulled up into the red dirt patch just off their front porch, Troy's mom hopped out and went directly inside.

Troy didn't move.

It had been a wild week for them all. Seth had been suspected of illegal steroid use. Troy had been accused of being a pawn in the Falcons' scheme to steal the signals from opposing NFL teams. And both of them had to be cleared so that they could help the Falcons continue their march to the playoffs. At first the media frenzy worked against them, but ultimately Troy used an interview with Larry King to set things right.

Tomorrow they'd be back at it, Troy calling the plays so that Seth could adjust the Falcons' defense, making the team virtually unstoppable in much the same way as their junior league football team had been unstoppable in its own championship game.

But that didn't seem possible now.

Seeing his father, even for those brief minutes outside Seth's house, changed things for Troy. Suddenly none of it seemed to matter. Troy knew that wasn't true. He knew how deep and strong his dream of being a part of an NFL team now—and one day playing on a team himself—really was. He knew that in his head; but his heart, swollen and aching for the father he never knew, made even his lifelong dreams fade into the background.

Troy didn't know how long he sat there in the dark with the pine trees whispering overhead before the front door cracked open and a band of orange light fell out onto the porch. Without closing the door behind her, his mom shuffled down the steps and rapped her knuckle on the car's passenger side window.

Troy opened the door but didn't get out.

CHAPTER FIVE

"WHAT, MOM?" TROY ASKED, his voice dull.

"You've got a big day tomorrow," his mom said. "The Falcons need you. I've got about a hundred emails with media requests that we've got to make some decisions on. You need to come inside and get some sleep. How's that finger?"

Troy shrugged.

"Can I see it?" his mom asked.

Troy held out his throwing hand, wincing even though she held it gently, and clucked her tongue.

"Come inside, Troy," she said. "We need to put some ice on this, and you need to get to sleep."

"You said that already," Troy said.

His mom squatted down so that her eyes were level

with his. She gently let go of his hand and touched his shoulder. She spoke in a soft whisper. "You have to forget him, Troy. He's not part of our lives. I'm sorry."

Troy's eyes brimmed with tears, and he shook his head. "All this time you said he didn't care, Mom. You said he wasn't a father, but he didn't *know*."

"Honey," she said, softer still, her fingers trailing through his hair, "he knew. Believe me, he knew."

"You said it was *possible*," Troy said, his voice hot. "I heard you; you just said that."

"Troy, 'possible' is a huge word," she said, still stroking his head, her voice still soft. "It's possible that the world could stop spinning, but it won't. Your father can twist things around—he's tricky like that; he always was. I'm not surprised he became a lawyer."

"I want to see him," Troy said, crossing his arms and dipping his chin.

His mother's hand stiffened, and she pulled it back and stood up so that he couldn't see her face outside the glow of the car's overhead light.

"That's not going to happen," she said, her voice cold now. "You come inside. It's bedtime."

Troy sniffed hard and swept the tears from his face. He jumped out of the car and glared at her.

"No," he said, "I won't, and you can't make me. I'm going to see my father if I have to hitch a train to Chicago, and you can't stop me!"

"Troy!" she yelled.

Troy didn't care.

His feet were already moving, flying across the tops of the needle beds, weaving through the pines and into the pitch-black of the night.

CHAPTER SIX

FROM THE MIDDLE OF the woods, Troy thought of something and went back to his house—not to return, but to retrieve the football he used to throw at the tire that hung from a tree on the edge of the dirt patch in front of the house. Troy had collected the signatures of the entire Falcons offense; if he was going to really go somewhere, he didn't plan to go without it.

He found the ball just inside the shed, closing its door quietly, with one eye on his house, before heading back through the pines and out toward the tracks. Up the stony bank Troy climbed. After the total darkness of the woods, he could almost see the shiny metal tracks and their straight path due north to Chicago or south to Atlanta, depending on your direction. Troy

15

headed south—not to Atlanta, but to the Pine Grove Apartments where both Nathan and Tate lived. It was Tate's apartment he went to, scooping up a handful of pebbles from the landscaping and tossing them up at the second-floor window he knew was hers.

It took a dozen stones before her light went on and the window slid open.

"Who's there?" Tate said, hissing into the night, just the edge of her face appearing between the curtains and the window frame.

"Tate," Troy said, "it's me."

Tate stuck her head right out the window then and, looking down, still whispering, asked, "What in the world are you doing?"

"Can you come down?" he asked.

Tate swept her long brown hair behind her ears and said, "You really need me to? It's, like, almost midnight."

"I do," he said.

"Okay," she said with a forceful nod, "let me get out of these pajamas."

Troy circled the apartment building and waited in the shadows until Tate's form slipped free from her front door and down the steps. She held a finger to her lips, and they stayed quiet until they reached the railroad tracks in back.

"Are you crazy?" Tate asked, still whispering.

"You don't have to whisper," Troy said.

"Who doesn't whisper?" Tate asked. "It's the middle of the night. The last time we did something like this, you almost got gunned down by a security guard inside Cotton Wood."

"I didn't almost get gunned down," Troy said.

"He *had* a gun."

"You sound like Nathan," Troy said.

"Where is Nathan?" she asked.

Troy shrugged. "I needed to talk to you. A woman's perspective, I guess."

Tate went silent for a minute, and they began walking down the tracks before she asked, "About your mom and your dad?"

"I ran away," Troy said.

"From home?"

"I guess."

"You can't do that," Tate said, upset.

"Now you sound like her," Troy said, smacking the ball he held with his free hand, then firing it at the trees beside the tracks so that it took off like a rocket, nearly straight up into the air, "telling me what to do, treating me like a little kid when I'm not. I'm making ten thousand dollars *a week*. And now with me being cleared by the NFL to help the Falcons, agents are coming out of the woodwork wanting to negotiate a deal for me with the Falcons or even another team for *millions*. Think about that, Tate. Millions."

"Well," she said, staring up at the tree toward which

Troy had thrown his ball, "at least you can afford to buy yourself another ball."

"What?" Troy said, following her gaze.

"That thing never came down," she said.

"It had to," Troy said, starting for the big pine tree.

"I didn't hear it," she said, following him.

"Me neither," he said, mumbling and searching the ground beneath the tree.

Tate stared up and said, "It's stuck."

"I got that signed by the entire Falcons offense," he said. "I need to get it."

Tate sighed and spit on her hands, heading for the trunk of the enormous pine tree.

"What are you doing?" he asked.

"I'll get it," she said, annoyed.

Troy watched her shinny up the trunk and scramble into the tree's branches. She shook one branch wildly, and the ball came tumbling down. It landed with a thump before bouncing crazily around and rolling down into the ditch beside the tracks. The branches shook as Tate moved into sight, then hung from the lowest branch and dropped down beside him as easy as if she were a cat.

"How'd you do that?" he asked.

Tate just shrugged and said, "A woman of many talents."

"You're like a lemur, Tate," Troy said, retrieving the ball from the ditch before climbing up onto the tracks, "but thanks. I wouldn't want to run away without this."

Troy turned to go, but Tate stopped him, and he could see her dark eyes glinting, even in the faintest light. "You just said you 'ran away.' That's what little kids do, not grown men."

"My father was a grown man," Troy said, swatting her hand away. "She says he ran away. I guess I'm like him. Anyway, I want to find him. If she doesn't want me, I can go live with him."

CHAPTER SEVEN

"WHOA," SHE SAID. "I know you took some shots in that game, but I didn't know it scrambled your brains completely."

"Why couldn't I?" Troy asked. "He seemed like a good guy."

"Troy, you met the man for about three minutes," Tate said.

"He had a pretty nice car," Troy said, then quickly added, "and he got into Cotton Wood because he said he had a client there. He must be pretty legit to have a client in Cotton Wood. Those people are all rich."

"You know what I'm saying," Tate said, stopping on the tracks. "Where are we going, Troy?"

"I don't know," Troy said. "The bridge?"

"It's pitch-black," Tate said with a shiver. "And it's

cold. I don't want to go far. You should go home. Really, you can't just run away. Think about it. I know you're mad. I know you want to see your dad."

"I *will* see my dad," Troy said.

Tate nodded her head. "I think so, too."

"You do?"

"Yes," Tate said. "He's your dad, Troy. He looks like you, and if he acts anything like you at all, then he's not just going to disappear. But you go home now, Troy. Trust me."

Troy gripped Tate's arm. "I do trust you, Tate. I know that no matter what, I can count on you. Best friends?"

"Best friends forever," Tate said, grinning.

Suddenly there was a noise in the bushes along the tracks: snapping branches and a guttural growling. Troy felt his heart jump into his throat.

"Oh my God," Tate said. "What is it?"

A figure burst out of the underbrush and bolted up the railway bed.

"Sheesh," Nathan said, swiping sweat from his brow. "Talk about a third wheel. All this best-friends stuff and I'm not even in on it?"

Then Nathan laughed to show he wasn't serious, and they joined him.

"You scared the stuffing out of me," Tate said. "Why are you crawling through the bushes?"

"My dad stayed late to help Seth pick up after the

party, and I saw you guys disappearing around the building when we pulled in," Nathan said. "I had to go out through my bedroom window, and I took the short-cut to catch you. What's up?"

Troy told Nathan what had happened. He nodded and agreed that Troy should go home.

"We all should," Tate said. "You okay, Troy?"

Troy nodded, and they all said good-bye. By the time he slipped in through the front door, the clock on the wall showed that it was just before one. He took a deep breath and tiptoed across the floor. With his mom, it was always best to work through things in the morn-ing. Without putting on the lights, Troy crept down the short hall to his bedroom, eased the door shut behind him, then flipped on the light. He breathed easier, smug with his strategy.

Then he turned around, and screamed.

CHAPTER EIGHT

"MOM, WHAT ARE YOU doing!" Troy yelled, the blast of fear still burning through his veins.

His mom sat upright against the headboard of his bed with her arms folded and her legs crossed, wearing a robe over her pajamas. She uncrossed her legs and swung them over the side, standing, but keeping her arms folded tight as if against some unknown chill.

"Waiting," she said, the word dropping from her lips like a stone.

"Well," Troy said, turning to his Xbox controller and winding up its cord, something he never did.

His mom brushed past him and left the room. From the hall she said, "I left two more of those pain pills for your finger on the table next to your bed. One for tonight and one for tomorrow, and don't forget to brush your teeth."

Then he heard her bedroom door close.

Troy shook his head and took the pain pill, brushed his teeth and went to bed. He lay awake. At first his finger throbbed out the rhythm of his heartbeat, but then the gentle wave of the pain pill softened the ache in his finger and his heart. He dropped off to sleep thinking of Tate's words about his father.

Troy ached more in the morning than he could ever remember. His whole body felt stiff and sore from the rough game they'd played, and his finger had blown up like a deli pickle. For a moment the whole thing—the championship, the agents who'd approached him in the parking lot, and even his father's appearance at Seth's house—all seemed like a dream. He took the second pain pill his mom had laid out with a glass of water beside his bed. Then he heard the sound of his grandfather's voice from the kitchen, and he jumped up and nearly tripped pulling on his pants as he swung open the door.

"Gramps!" Troy said, hugging his grandfather where he sat at the kitchen table. "Where were you last night?"

"I was there for the game, are you kidding?" Gramps said. "But I'm too old for parties. Besides, that was for your team. No, I just went home afterward and had a cup of tea on my porch to celebrate."

His grandfather, tough and straight as an old stick, wore wire-rimmed glasses that highlighted his blazing pale blue eyes. His hair was mostly gone, and on his chin he had a white stubble that could leave a raspberry on Troy's skin. As Troy stepped back, Gramps held out one iron hand.

"Give me the grip," he said, then he looked at Troy's swollen finger. "Ouch. Better not. I saw them messing with you on the sideline and that last pass that looked like a dead duck, but I didn't know you messed yourself up this bad."

"I'm okay," Troy said.

Troy's mom turned away from the stove with platters of eggs, grits, and sausages, setting them out on the table before taking a pitcher of orange juice from the fridge and then pouring herself and her father cups of steaming hot coffee.

"The doctor said the finger isn't broken," Troy's mom said, blowing on her coffee and looking from Troy to Gramps over the rim of the mug. "It's his heart I'm worried about, Dad."

Gramps shoveled some food onto his plate and said, "Sounds serious. Girl trouble? That Tate McGreer turned him down?"

"Gramps," Troy said, nearly choking on his juice, "Tate's my friend. I don't have a girlfriend."

"She's a cutie, though," Gramps said, a twinkle in

his eye as he mixed the eggs and grits together with some sausage before taking a big bite.

"Drew showed up, Dad," Troy's mom said, her voice cold enough to wipe the smile off Gramps's face.

"Oh?" Gramps said, swallowing. "Showed up? Where do you mean? After the game?"

"He saw us on *Larry King*, Gramps," Troy said. "He said he didn't know I even existed, and Mom said that was possible."

Gramps tilted his head down and looked at Troy's mom over the top of his glasses. "She did?"

"I said 'possible,' Dad," Troy's mom said, "but lots of things are possible. I figured if anyone could explain to Troy why you can't just show up twelve years into a boy's life and expect to be some kind of inflatable father figure, it would be you. You've been more of a father to him than the fathers a lot of kids have."

Gramps sipped his mug of coffee and rubbed the bristles on his chin. "I've enjoyed spending time with Troy. Not much at cleaning fish, but he sure catches 'em well enough."

Gramps winked at Troy.

"I'm serious, Dad," Troy's mom said. "I told Drew to leave us alone. I don't want him treating Troy like a yo-yo."

"Well," Gramps said softly. "It's a tough thing Troy's been through. Oh, I know you've done everything a mom could do, Tessa; and I guess I have, too. But it's different, a boy and his dad."

"See, Mom?" Troy said, excited at the direction in which things were headed.

"Still," Gramps said, turning his blazing eyes on Troy, "your mom has a point. You're at that in-between time of life, Troy. You're not a kid anymore, but you're not quite a man. It's a hard time, and I think maybe, if your dad really means what he says, well, when you're a man he'll still be there, and the two of you can get acquainted and see where it goes. Jumping in on the parent wagon at this point doesn't do anyone much good."

"Gramps," Troy said, standing so fast that his chair fell over, "I can't believe you're taking her side. I took off last night, and I should have stayed gone."

CHAPTER NINE

"HEY, MISTER," **HIS MOM** said, raising her voice and banging her mug so that coffee splashed out onto the tabletop. "I thought we were over that. I let it slide; now you're tossing it in my face?"

"What am I tossing?" Troy said, bending to flip the chair upright before backing away toward his bedroom. "I've always dreamed I had a dad. I knew he was out there, somewhere. Now he found me. Do you know how good that feels?"

"For now," she said, standing up. "For the moment."

"Why? Why just for the moment?" Troy asked.

"Because I know him, Troy," she said, her hands clasped and her voice almost pleading. "You don't. You saw him pull up in a hundred-thousand-dollar car with a fancy pair of cowboy boots. I know who he is, and I

28

know what he did—to both of us."

"You always say 'forgive and forget,'" Troy said. "What about that? That's only for when it's good for you? What about now? Why can't *you* forgive?"

"Okay, I forgive him," she said, "fine. That's not what this is about. I do forgive him, but I don't want to let him hurt us again—hurt *you*."

"I don't *care* if I get hurt," Troy said, trying not to shout. "I'm hurt already. You don't know what it's like to have people look at you, the kid without a dad. The football player without a dad."

"Don't tell me I don't know," she said, shaking her head so that her hair lay in a crazed web on her shoulders. "I know. I'm the woman with no husband, the woman with a broken family and a troubled son."

"I'm not troubled!" Troy yelled.

"You just said you were!"

"STOP!"

Troy and his mom froze. Gramps was on his feet now, too, and it was the first time Troy had ever heard him shout.

"Now," Gramps said in his normal voice, his hands motioning for them both to sit and settle down. "Both of you. Sit down. We're all on the same side here. We are. And, if you'll listen, I think I've got a solution."

CHAPTER TEN

"THERE ARE LAWS," **GRAMPS** said, "that give your father some rights."

"Dad!" Troy's mom said, her lips curling back in disgust.

"You need to listen, young lady," Gramps said, his voice and look stern. "It's true. Drew has rights. If he can show he didn't know about Troy and he's his father, the court will give him some kind of visitation rights, especially if Troy wants it."

Troy's mom bit her lip and winced.

"And," Gramps said, turning his eyes on Troy, "your mom can fight it. She can get a good lawyer and drag this thing out so that it'd be years before Drew could ever see you.

"That wouldn't be good," Gramps said. "But, Troy,

you have to know this. Your father is a smart man. If he really wants to see you, to be a part of your life, then he'll find the laws if he doesn't know them already. And, if he's willing to use his time and money and initiate a suit, then I say it proves he's not just showing up on a whim because he saw you two on *Larry King*. That's what I say."

Gramps picked up his fork and rammed home a mouthful of food, chewing so that his leathery neck danced up and down and side to side.

"He has to sue to get to see me?" Troy asked in disbelief.

"No," his mom said softly, "that's not what Gramps is saying. He's saying that *if* it's that important to Drew to see you, then he'll begin a lawsuit, *and* if he does, we'll just settle it right out of the gate."

"Why do we have to make it hard on him?" Troy asked.

Gramps held up his hand so Troy's mom would let him speak. He swallowed and washed down the mouthful with a gulp of juice before he said, "Because he made it hard on you, Troy. And on your mom. There's a saying that anything worth having is worth fighting for, and it's true. If he really wants a relationship, let him fight for it. Then when he does get it, he's a lot less apt to walk away from it."

"Again," Troy's mom said.

Gramps glared at her.

"Well?" she said to Gramps before dropping her shoulders and turning to Troy. "Okay, I'm sorry. I'll behave."

His mom extended her hand across the table and let it hang there between them.

"Is it a deal, Troy?" she asked.

CHAPTER ELEVEN

"SO," TROY SAID, EYEING her hand, "we don't do anything, but if my dad says he's going to start a lawsuit to try to get visitation rights, then you let me see him?"

"That's right," his mom said. "Let him make the first move. Gramps is right. If he *really* wants to be your dad. If he's really sorry and he's going to be in it for the long haul, then he's not just going to go away, Troy."

"Okay," Troy said, nodding his head and clasping her hand. "Deal."

Gramps smacked his hands together and rubbed them as if he were trying to get warm. "Nice, now let's get serious about this breakfast. These eggs remind me of Waffle House back in Avondale, before it was a chain."

Troy smiled and dug in. They ate for a bit, recounting

the highlights of the championship game, Troy's touchdown passes, especially the final, ugly lob to Nathan, who had been wide open in the end zone on a trick play.

"Gramps," Troy said, "how come you didn't stick around?"

Gramps wiped his mouth and swished his hand through the air. "I saw you surrounded by all those cameras and all; I'm too old for a mess like that. I knew I'd see you this morning and congratulate you proper. You, my friend, played like a champion, and you are a champion. To the bone."

Gramps raised his orange juice glass.

Troy blushed and looked at his plate. "Thanks, Gramps."

"Did you see the agents, Dad?" Troy's mom asked.

"The who?" Gramps asked, his forehead rumpling beneath his bald dome.

"Agents," Troy's mom said. "They practically swarmed us after the interviews."

"I was gone by then," he said. "What did 'agents' want?"

"To represent me, Gramps," Troy said, suddenly excited at the recollection of the men in suits handing him and his mom their cards. "One of them, some Nash guy, he said I could get between one and two million."

"Two million what?" Gramps asked.

"Dollars, Gramps," Troy said. "We could all be rich."

Gramps's face fell. "Rich? I don't know about that. A couple of people I know who got rich don't do so well with it. It's overrated."

Troy stared at Gramps.

"Dad," Troy's mom said.

"Of course, it's not always bad," Gramps said, swigging some coffee with a nod. "You can take some pretty nice vacations with two million dollars. Educational things like the rain forest or the Galápagos Islands. Maybe Antarctica."

"How about a new pickup truck, Gramps?"

"Oh, no. I'm fine. Nothing I need."

"Well," Troy's mom said, "either way, we'll need an agent. Let's get today's game behind us, and tomorrow I'll start to set up some meetings so we can figure out who to go with. I want to try and keep your life as normal as possible, Troy. A good agent can even handle the media for us, be a buffer."

"Buffer?"

"A barrier," his mom said, "between you and the teams, you and the media, all the outside distractions. You still need to go to school, have your friends, play your football."

"Well," Troy said, "football's over for now anyway."

His mom raised an eyebrow. "Seth didn't tell you?"

"Tell me what?"

CHAPTER TWELVE

"WE LEFT SO FAST last night," Troy's mom said. "I guess that was my fault. He wanted to tell you before he made a general announcement, so no one knows."

"Tell me what, Mom?"

"No, you'll have to wait until you see him," she said. "I know he wants to be the one to tell you."

"Mom, you can't do this."

"Nope," his mom said, making a locking motion on her lips and pretending to throw away the key.

Troy jumped up and grabbed the phone on the wall. "I'll call him."

"Don't," his mom said. "Since the game isn't until four today, he's sleeping in. You'll see him at the stadium."

"Meantime," Gramps said, rising from the table,

tugging free the necktie he'd hung on the back of the chair and looping it around his head, "we got church, so get yourself changed."

"Do I have to go?" Troy asked. "I just won the championship."

"All the more reason *to* go," Gramps said, winking. "You don't think that last pass ended up in Nathan's hands just because of you, do you?"

They all laughed.

Troy got changed and so did his mom.

When they got home from church, Troy put on his Falcons gear, happy to be free from the stiff shirt with its collar and tie. Gramps headed home to watch the game on TV, something he did as religiously as going to church.

"How's the finger?" Troy's mom asked when she emerged from her bedroom with the clipboard she used for work.

Troy looked at his injured finger, tried to move it, and winced.

"Not good."

His mom looked at her watch and said, "Might be time for another pain pill."

"I know," Troy said, "but I was thinking, Mom. The pills work, but they make me kind of light-headed. I mean, with everything going so well—me getting my job back, the Falcons on this playoff run, and all these agents talking about me making a ton of money—I just don't know if I should take the chance of being foggy. What if the pain pill keeps me from being able to see the patterns?"

His mom looked at him for a minute and pressed her lips together. "Well, what if the discomfort keeps you from being able to see the patterns?"

"If the pain bothers me that much," Troy said, "and I can't get with it, then I can always take the pill then."

His mom nodded. "Good idea. I hate to think of you suffering, though."

"Part of the game, right?" Troy said, trying to smile.

His mom sighed and nodded.

They picked up Tate and Nathan on their way to the Georgia Dome. Mr. Langan had given permission for Troy's two best friends to be on the sideline with him during the game, so long as they didn't distract him.

They got to park in the staff lot and go in through the same entrance as the players. Troy still couldn't get over the size of the men walking past. They were giants in all kinds of clothes—from sweats or jeans to suits and ties—with hands the size of hubcaps and heads like upside-down buckets. They all recognized Troy and gave him anything from a clap on the back to a wink and a thumbs-up. Most of them congratulated Troy on winning the junior league state championship. Troy blushed at the attention but had to admit to himself that he enjoyed it.

Tate and Nathan silently accepted passes to the sideline from Troy's mom and strung them through the belt loops in their jeans. Both wore Falcons shirts and hats like Troy.

Troy and his friends followed Troy's mom out onto the field. With more than two hours to go before game time, no one was in the dome except for the players from both the Falcons and the visiting Green Bay Packers. Aside from the hum of the lights suspended from the web of steel above, the place was strangely quiet. A handful of players already covered the field, stretching out and warming up in football pants and T-shirts. Troy's mom showed Nathan and Tate where they could sit and wait on the bench while Troy went into the locker room to meet with Seth and the coaches.

When Troy walked into the meeting room just off the side of the locker room, he was disappointed to see that both Coach McFadden, the head coach, and Jim Mora, the defensive coordinator, were already sitting there beside Seth. Troy ached to ask Seth about the surprise his mother only hinted about but knew it would have to wait. Together, the four of them discussed the process for getting the correct calls to Seth during the game. It usually took Troy at least a couple of series of plays to see the patterns that told him the opponent's game plan. He would stand next to Coach Mora until that time came. The instant it did, he could describe the play, and the coach could signal the correct defensive call to Seth. Troy didn't want to even tell them about how badly his finger hurt, because there was nothing they could do about it anyway. He could only hope that it wouldn't keep him from using his gift.

When the meeting broke up, Troy tried to get Seth's attention, but Coach Mora put an arm around the star linebacker, and the two of them headed back into the locker room. Troy put a hand on the door but hesitated. The door swung open, and Coach McFadden appeared, asking Troy if he wanted to walk out onto the field with him. Troy did, and it wasn't long before the two of them were wandering the turf, talking to the individual players. Most of the team was out on the field by now, and Coach McFadden seemed to have words of encouragement for even the backup players. It wasn't until the head coach began a conversation with Mr. Langan that Troy saw Seth jogging slowly up the sideline with a headset on, playing his music.

Troy slipped away and intercepted Seth near the Falcons bench.

"Hey, buddy," Seth said, slipping the earphones down around his neck and pausing the music.

"You okay?" Troy asked, nodding at Seth's knees, which Troy knew had grown increasingly worse as the season progressed.

Seth made a face, then said, "Part of it. I'll get warmed up and be okay. Got the left one drained and took a little cortisone. I'll get by. It's always tough later in the season. What about you, buddy? You feeling good? How's that finger? It looks like junk."

"I took a pain pill this morning," Troy said, flexing his finger stiffly.

"Well, look brave," Seth said, angling his head toward the field. A cameraman with a handheld camera and an assistant holding the cable were moving their way with the camera pointed at Troy. "You're on."

"I thought the media wasn't allowed inside the yellow rope," Troy said.

"That's the FOX game camera. The NFL lets one network cameraman inside the yellow, and that's him," Seth said. "You want me to make him go away?"

Troy had nothing against being on TV, so he shook his head. The cameraman came right up to him and Seth, moving the lens back and forth just inches from their faces. The thought of being on TV brought back the nervousness he'd felt on *Larry King Live*, and Troy could only stand there as stiff as a ruler.

"Troy?" the cameraman asked. "You two going to put one on the Packers today?"

Troy forced a smile and gave a thumbs-up.

"Seth," the cameraman said, "how's it feel knowing what the other team is going to do before they do?"

"Well," Seth said, slinging an arm around Troy's shoulder, "I wouldn't say it's before they know, but it's not too long after. You still gotta make the play, though, right? It's not chess; it's still football."

"Great," the cameraman said with a nod, moving on toward some other players.

"I felt so goofy," Troy said, watching them go.

"You'll get used to it," Seth said, flicking a finger at the brim of Troy's hat so it tipped back on his head.

"Seth, my mom said you've got something to tell me? She said the season might not be over? I mean, we won the championship. There's nothing after that, right?"

Seth broke out into a huge grin. "That's what I thought." He nodded over at where Tate and Nathan sat on the bench. "Come on, let me tell the three of you together. You're all going to be a part of it."

"It's something good, my mom said." Troy's palms were actually sweating with anticipation.

"No," Seth said, "it's something great."

CHAPTER THIRTEEN

THE DOORS TO THE dome had been opened, and fans had begun to trickle in, their excited talk washing over the hum of the lights. Troy knew that the entire city of Atlanta had been electrified by the Falcons late-season run at the playoffs, led by their favorite star, Seth Halloway.

Troy followed Seth over to the bench, where the star linebacker greeted Nathan and Tate.

"So," Seth said, "I've got some good news for all three of you. It's something I wasn't even aware of, being a latecomer to this junior league coaching thing. The other night, one of the state league officials let me know about this thing they call the Border War."

"Border War?" Troy said.

"Georgia versus Florida," Seth said. "It's a tradition.

This Saturday, when the SEC has their championship game in the Georgia Dome, they host an all-star game between the best junior league players from Georgia and Florida. It's on the morning of the big game. The coaches from both colleges watch from the sidelines, too. Good way to get on their radar screen for early recruiting."

"We play against kids from Florida?" Nathan asked. "The Duluth Tigers?"

"Not the Tigers," Seth said. "It's an all-star team. All the best junior league players in Georgia get put on the same team to go against the best kids in Florida."

"And we're on the team?" Tate asked.

"If you want to be," Seth said. "I'm the coach, and since we won the championship, they told me I could bring my four best players. That's you three, plus Rusty Howell."

Troy was the heart of the championship team and could throw as well as anyone his age. Nathan was one of the biggest twelve-year-olds on the planet and had anchored the Duluth Tigers' line. Tate had already won the regional punt, pass, and kick competition with her powerful leg. Rusty was Troy's top receiver and the fastest kid any of them knew.

"Of course we want to," Troy said. "This is great!"

"Who else is on the team?" Nathan asked.

Seth said, "Valdosta got to name three players since they were second in the state. The other top ten each got to name two players, and then there are about a dozen others from all over. And, get this, everyone who plays gets a scholarship."

"Scholarship?" Tate asked.

"Five thousand dollars," Seth said, nodding, "and ten thousand if we win it. It's good for any college you end up going to. We'll be having practices during your Thanksgiving vacation, though. So, you guys in?"

"Of course!"

"Yes!"

"For sure!"

"Okay," Seth said, "I told you it was great news. Our first practice is Tuesday night. Now, I gotta get going here. I don't want you guys to be the only champs around town."

They all wished him good luck, and Seth put his headphones back on before continuing his jog around the field. The three of them talked excitedly about the Border War and playing against Florida's all-stars right there in the Georgia Dome. When Tate and Nathan started to talk about the scholarship money, Troy kept quiet and could only think about the money he was already making as the Falcons football genius and how it sometimes didn't seem real.

As the dome began to fill up, people also filtered out onto the sidelines. A long bright yellow rope ran from one post to another, marking the area on the sideline where only the players, coaches, and team employees were allowed to go. Outside, media and VIP guests of the team were allowed to watch the warm-ups and to speak to the players who wandered near.

When the three of them ambled up the sideline to watch the Falcons' receivers practice one-handed catches, Troy was surprised to hear his name being called from somewhere behind the yellow rope. He took a quick glance and recognized the face of a man with spiked blond hair who wore dark sunglasses with flashy rims and what looked like a bicycle chain made of gold with a platinum thousand-dollar bill dangling from it.

"That's G Money," Troy said without thinking.

Nathan and Tate stopped and stared.

"Cool," Nathan said. "Gangsta rap. I just got his new CD; it's, like, his fourth one to go platinum."

"What's he doing here?" Tate asked.

"He's big-time," Nathan said.

"What about all the rumors that he's still part of that gang from Chicago?" Tate asked. "Look at that other guy. Is that a jaguar tattooed on his neck?"

Troy saw the enormous man who stood just behind G Money. He was as big as the NFL linemen, with a bald pink head and rimless, rectangular eyeglass frames. His small right ear was a tattered mess, but Troy barely noticed it past the rolls of fat on his neck and the deadly stare of his cold blue eyes. On his face he wore a thick, furry beard, rounded like a cartoon character's and giving no sign of the mouth behind it.

"Aw," Nathan said, swatting at the air, "you watch too much TV. That's all an act."

"I don't know," Tate said under her breath. "That guy's scary."

"Seth took me by G Money's house in Cotton Wood once," Troy said. "It's the biggest mansion in that place, a huge white thing with columns as tall as telephone poles."

"Hey," Tate said, pointing not toward G Money but to the man standing on the opposite side of him from the big guy.

"Troy!" the man called, waving his hand for Troy to come over.

"Oh my God," Troy said, the blood rushing to his brain.

"That's my dad."

CHAPTER FOURTEEN

TROY APPROACHED THE YELLOW rope, his heart swelling with pride. Gramps and his mom said if his father truly wanted a relationship, he wouldn't give up; and showing up on the Falcons' sideline certainly wasn't giving up. It wasn't a lawsuit, but to Troy it looked good enough to count for that "first move" his mom had spoken about.

"Let me introduce you and your friends," Troy's dad said, dipping under the rope and tugging G Money along with him, leaving the scary guy behind.

A security guard in a yellow Windbreaker hollered and headed their way. Troy's dad wore a trim double-breasted suit with a shiny blue tie. His hair had been styled with gel, and on one of his wrists he wore a slim gold watch that glittered with diamonds. He looked slick.

"Sir," the security guard said, "I'm sorry but—"

"Relax," Troy's dad said smoothly. "I'm with G Money. I'm his lawyer. This is my son, the football genius everyone's talking about. His mom's the PR director. We're good."

The security guard looked at G Money's smile and blinked at the shiny gold grille on his teeth. He nodded his head and backed away.

"Dad, she's not the PR director," Troy said under his breath.

His dad waved a hand as if he were shooing flies and said, "Your buddies from last night, right? Kids, this is G Money. I'm his personal lawyer. I do all his deals, right, G?"

"You're my homey, Drew," G said, bumping fists. "And I heard about you, little man, helping my team. I grew up about three blocks from this stadium. Love the Falcons, so you rock."

Troy bumped fists with the famous rapper, using his left hand because of his hurt finger. Jimmy Cribbs, the team photographer, appeared from nowhere and said, "Mr. Money, how about a picture with you and Troy? A music genius and a football genius, both huge Falcons fans."

"You got it," G said, slinging his arm around Troy.

Troy's dad got into the picture on the other side of G, winked at Troy, and gave him a thumbs-up. Troy beamed with pride as the camera flashed, and he asked if his friends could get in a picture as well.

"For sure," Troy's dad said. "G loves kids, don't you, G."

"You the man, Drew," G said.

Drew put his arm around Troy and steered him off to the side a bit so he could speak privately into Troy's ear. "You hear that? See, I do everything important for him—his contracts, his investments, all his deals. When you're big-time like G, there are about a billion people coming at you from about a million different directions. It's not easy, believe me."

"So you're, like, his agent?" Troy asked.

"Agent?" Drew said, touching fingertips to his chest. "Don't insult me."

"Sorry," Troy said.

His dad laughed, mussed Troy's hair, and said, "Agents are cheese balls, salesmen. I told you, G's big-time. The big-time people all have *lawyers*. That's me."

"Wow," Troy said, feeling silly after the word got loose. "Last night, it sounded like you wanted to see me."

"I do," Drew said. "I'm your father."

Troy's whole body tingled at the sound of the word.

"I probably shouldn't be telling you this," Troy said, glancing around to make sure no one could hear. "You have to sue her."

"What?" his father asked.

"Sue her," Troy said in an urgent whisper. "A lawsuit.

If you do, she'll let me see you."

"That's what she said?" his father asked with a look of disbelief.

"She wants you to prove you're serious," Troy said, "but I know you are. I know because you're *here*. You came to see me, right?"

"Of course," his dad said, showing Troy his empty palms. "G's got the keys to the city, but I was the one who pushed him to come here today because I knew he could get us passes. But tell me, why did you ask about agents? I'm curious."

Pride bubbled up in Troy's chest. "I've got agents who want to represent *me*."

"Agents?" his dad said. "For what?"

Troy's smile faltered. "Well—didn't you hear? This football genius thing. They say I could get—I don't know—millions for it."

"Millions?" his father said, rubbing his chin. "I don't know about that."

Troy glanced around, lowered his voice, and said, "The Falcons are paying me ten thousand a week right now."

"That's great," his father said, but with enthusiasm that was obviously forced. "Good for you, Troy. I bet you pay your share of the grocery bills with that."

"I want to buy my mom a car," Troy said, frustrated, "and one day a house in Cotton Wood."

"Cotton Wood?" his dad said, chuckling. "In G's neighborhood?"

"Well," Troy said, "one day. Yes."

"Uh," his dad said, looking past Troy and angling his head, "speaking of your mother? Here she comes."

CHAPTER FIFTEEN

"**I TOLD YOU,**" **TROY'S** mom said to Drew, her face pinched with anger.

"Hey," Drew said, raising his hands in mock surrender, "I'm just here with my client. Troy and his buddies wanted some pictures."

"Your *client*?" Troy's mom said, looking around and seeing G Money signing the back of Nathan's hand with a permanent marker. "That guy?"

"That 'guy' has four platinum records," Drew said, "and he made about twenty million dollars last year."

"That doesn't impress me," Troy's mom said, her mouth a flat line. "You don't have a pass for this area. Either of you. You'll have to step back outside the yellow line. You and Jiminy, or whoever he is."

"G Money," Drew said with a smirk. "The kids know who he is."

"The kids aren't in charge here," Troy's mom said. "I am."

"You want to put me in handcuffs?" his dad said with nasty sarcasm, holding out his wrists. "Even though G and I are guests of the mayor?"

Troy felt like a fly jiggling in a web built by two spiders as they traded angry words.

"Well, that's good news about the mayor," Troy's mom said, signaling one of the security guards. "At least we know that the paper's charges of corruption probably aren't completely unfounded. But now it's time to do what you do best, Drew . . . leave."

"You got it, Tessa," his dad said. "You're right. You're in charge. For now."

Troy's mom nodded and raised the rope. Drew and G Money ducked back outside it. The big man waited for them like a mountain, only his dark eyes following the action.

Once Troy's dad stood on the other side, he said, "I hate to do this, Tessa, but you're leaving me no choice."

Troy's mom asked, "No choice for what?"

CHAPTER SIXTEEN

"IF YOU DON'T WORK with me here, I'm going to have to sue you," Drew said. "For partial custody of Troy. I think a boy needs a dad. I don't know about the laws here in Georgia, but, believe me, I'm going to look into it, and you can expect to hear from my lawyer."

"I thought you were a lawyer," Troy's mom said with a smirk of her own.

"Any lawyer who represents himself has a fool for a client," Drew said. "Haven't you heard that saying, Tessa? Well, I'm no fool. Far from it."

Troy's father gave him a secret wink, then took a business card from his wallet and clamped it between two fingers like a cigarette before extending it to Troy.

"In case he needs to get in touch with me," Drew said, raising an eyebrow at Troy's mom, "and you decide you'd like to settle this in a nice way. I'm in town until tomorrow night, and I'd like to take Troy out to lunch or Six Flags or something before I go. That okay with you, Tessa?"

Troy reached hesitantly for the card, looking at her. "Mom?"

His mom clenched her teeth, her eyes darting between them.

"You said," Troy said to her in a low voice.

A thin stream of air escaped between her teeth before she said, "Not now, Troy. You've got school. I have to think. *I'll* take the card."

Before Troy could protest, his mom snatched the card from Drew and said, "Okay, Troy. You've got things to do, right?"

Troy scowled at his mom as she steered him back toward the center of the bench area, where, in fact, Coach Mora was looking for him. As they went, Troy glanced over his shoulder. Nathan was still talking to G from inside the yellow rope, and Tate stood beside him. Troy's dad motioned to Troy, jacked up his eyebrows, and pointed with quick, stabbing motions at Tate. Before Tate could do anything about it, Drew reached over the rope, took her hand, and slapped another one of his business cards into it before closing her fingers around it and propelling her gently toward Troy.

"Troy, I'll leave you with Coach Mora. We'll talk

about that other thing later," Troy's mom said before moving on to her PR duties.

Troy tried to pay attention to the questions Coach Mora asked him, but he could only give simple yes or no answers. With Tate now standing beside him, Troy's skin felt tight, and his fingers were itching to snatch his father's business card out of her pocket and make it his own.

"You okay?" Coach Mora asked.

"Fine," Troy said.

"You coming into the locker room with us for the pre-game speech?" Coach Mora asked. The players behind him had begun to vacate the field, moving in a large bunch toward the locker room.

"I think I'll wait with these guys on the bench if it's okay," Troy said.

"Sure," Coach Mora said, turning to go. "See you for the national anthem."

Troy looked back toward where his father had been, but both he and G—along with all the other guests— had been cleared off the sideline by a wave of security guards in yellow Windbreakers. The last of them were being funneled out the visiting team's tunnel entrance like used dishwater down a drain.

Troy held out his hand to Tate and said, "Let me have it."

Tate seemed reluctant to give up the card. She said, "I feel like I'm in the middle of this. Your mom didn't want you to have it."

"Whose side are you on?" Troy asked, the words sounding nastier than he'd intended.

Tate's face turned red, and her fingers curled around the card so that it crumpled in her hand. "No side, that's my point. I don't think it's fair, making me the delivery girl when your mom doesn't want you to have this."

"You act like it's stolen property or something, Tate," Troy said. "Cut it out. He's my dad. Let go."

Troy gripped her wrist with his hurt hand and pried the card loose with the other.

"What the heck?" he said, tearing it free, the struggle causing him pain.

"Good," Tate said, relieved. "Now if it comes out, I didn't *give* it to you. You took it from me."

"Whatever," Troy said, studying the card, then looking up at the luxury boxes above them, wondering which one belonged to the mayor.

"Whatever?" Tate said. "Your mom is your mom, Troy."

"And my dad is my dad."

"Okay," Tate said, still sour. "I get it."

With his good hand, Troy stuffed the card into his pocket and said, "I don't know; this whole thing's got me crazy."

"Well, it's all pretty unusual," Tate said.

"But who cares?" Nathan said. "Hanging out with G Money? That's worth some ruffled feathers, I gotta tell you. Look at that, right on my hand."

Nathan beamed as he held forth the hand G had signed.

"Permanent, too," Nathan said proudly. "It's *never* coming off."

"Nathan, the only thing permanent is a tattoo," Tate said.

"Wrong, Tate," Nathan said, scowling. "My mom said those Sharpies never come off."

"Maybe not off your dining-room table when you went outside the lines on that social studies poster we made," Tate said, "but it's not permanent on your hand."

"Dang!" Nathan said, then snapped his fingers and took out his phone.

"What are you doing?" Troy asked.

"A picture," Nathan said, showing them. "A picture of my hand signed by G Money. Now, that's forever."

"I don't care about G Money, or his autograph," Troy said, leading them over to the bench and flopping down with his legs extended. He smoothed out his father's business card and examined it. "Seven hundred and fifty-three Michigan Avenue. That sounds like a pretty fancy address to me."

"Michigan Avenue is where all the famous stores are in Chicago," Tate said, "and the Water Tower. It looks like a castle."

"Hey, if he's G Money's lawyer," Nathan said, brandishing his hand, "then he's got to be huge. You can't get more famous than G."

"Troy'll be that famous soon," Tate said. "We saw the TV camera on you and Seth, and I heard your mom saying something to another reporter about you maybe being at the team press conference after the game."

"She did?" Troy asked, his cheeks feeling warm.

"Maybe she doesn't want you to think about it," Tate said. "Maybe I shouldn't have mentioned it."

The three of them sat silently for a few minutes, the crowd in the dome continuing to grow, filling the seats and adding to the noise and the ocean of red and black.

Finally, Nathan said, "I know I'm not really the idea guy, but I can't stop thinking about this one."

Nathan waited, and neither Tate nor Troy said anything.

"Aren't one of you guys going to ask?" Nathan said.

Troy sighed and said, "Okay, Nathan. What?"

"Well, your dad's this big-time lawyer doing deals for people like G Money, right?" Nathan said.

"Yeah," Troy said.

"And you've got all these agents wanting to do your deal with the Falcons or even another NFL team after this season, right?"

"Yup."

"So," Nathan said, "why not forget the agents and—"

"I know what you're going to say," Troy said, holding up a hand to cut him off.

"You do?"

"Yes," Troy said, "because I'm sitting here thinking the exact same thing."

CHAPTER SEVENTEEN

"**WHAT SAME THING ARE** you two thinking?" Tate asked.

Nathan said, "That Troy's dad—"

"Can represent me," Troy said, finishing the sentence.

"Guys," Tate said, "you just met the man."

"It's his father, Tate," Nathan said, rolling his eyes.

"You think I'm blind?" Tate said. "He still just met the man. Troy doesn't even know him."

"He doesn't know any of these agents banging down his door either," Nathan said.

"He knows Seth," Tate said. "And Seth has an agent. Don't you think you'd want to be with someone you know you can t—"

"What?" Troy asked, glaring at Tate. "Trust? That's

what you were going to say, isn't it, Tate? Why wouldn't I trust my own father?"

Troy stared at her until Tate looked away.

"I'm sorry," she said. "I'll keep my mouth shut. Can we talk about all this later? I mean, you've got to help the Falcons win this game, right? We shouldn't be distracting you. Mr. Langan asked us not to, remember, Nathan?"

"I'm not distracting him," Nathan said, jabbing his thumb into his chest. "I'm helping him."

"I probably should get focused on the game," Troy said, realizing that less than three minutes remained on the clock before the team would come bursting through the smoke and flames at the mouth of the Falcons tunnel. "I'm not going to have to worry about contracts or agents or any of this if I can't keep helping them win. That's football, right? You're only as good as your last game. Come on, let's watch."

Troy buried the card in his left pocket. They got up and stood right on the broad white strip of sideline at the midpoint of the field. The dome began to rumble. The announcer's voice shouted out a welcome to the fans and introduced the Falcons' defensive starters one by one. The tunnel exploded with fresh flames as each defender burst from the tunnel at the sound of his name, sprinting past a double row of cheerleaders. Seth was the last defender to be announced, and he got the loudest cheers. The rest of the team came racing out of the tunnel behind him, accompanied by a surge of twenty-foot flames. The Falcons formed a twisting mass at the center of the field, shouting and jumping and hooting at the top of their lungs. Smoke floated toward the roof. The crowd went wild, and Troy and his friends had to plug their ears.

The team migrated to the bench area, but energy stayed high, even when the Falcons lost the coin toss. The fans cheered when the Packers chose to receive the kickoff. The entire crowd seemed eager to see Seth and the defense tear into the Packers with the help of their secret weapon who was no longer a secret. Troy stood next to Coach Mora at the edge of the sideline, while Tate and Nathan had to stay on the bench so they wouldn't get trampled. As the captains came off the field after the coin toss, the cameraman with the handheld camera jogged along behind them and practically stuck his lens in Troy's face. The red light went on, and Troy shifted on his feet and blushed.

"Oh, no," Coach Mora said, grabbing the cameraman by the shoulder and gently shoving him away. "You guys stay out of his face. He needs to work."

The cameraman disappeared up the sideline, outside the team's yellow line. The Falcons' kickoff team took the field. Seth appeared beside Troy, his eyes bugging out and a crazed smile plastered across his face.

"You ready, buddy?" Seth asked, holding up a taped fist.

"Yeah," Troy said. The word came out so quietly, he was sure Seth couldn't hear it amid all the noise, so he nodded his head.

The whistle sounded. The game began. The Falcons' kickoff team smashed the Packers' returner, pinning the visitors deep in their own territory.

The defense now took the field, and Troy put his hands on his knees and focused on Green Bay: on their offensive personnel, the body language of the different players, the formations, the motion, the action. After every play Coach Mora would glance at Troy expectantly, waiting for his genius to kick in. Usually it took eight to twelve plays before the patterns became clear. A couple of times over the past weeks, Troy's ability had been stifled by pressure, and once by a lingering headache after Troy took a shot to the head in one of his junior league games.

Having his father suddenly appear in his life had no doubt created some extra stress and tension, but after only five plays Troy broke into a huge grin.

"Screen pass left," Troy said to Mora.

Coach Mora gave him a startled look, then returned his smile before frantically signaling to Seth out on the field to let him know about the screen. Quickly, with a second series of hand signals, Mora told Seth to put the defense in a blanket zone coverage that would shut down any screen. Seth paused for a moment, then began shouting instructions to his fellow players that Troy couldn't make out. The Packers approached the line. The Falcons scrambled to their places. Troy looked back at his two friends. His mom stood there now as well, and he gave them all a thumbs-up before turning his attention back to the field.

The Packers ran exactly what Troy had predicted: a screen to the left.

But instead of the blanket zone Mora had called for, the Falcons' defense rushed with an all-out blitz, with most of the team gushing up through the line. Troy shot a look of disbelief at Mora, who winced in anger. The Packers' linemen let the Falcons' defense right through. The quarterback retreated, drawing them farther up the field like a pack of dogs mad for a rabbit. Only a handful of Falcons dropped into coverage. Seth stayed close to the line, floating toward the Packers' running back, who had pretended to fall down before getting up and sprinting for the sideline to catch the screen. Most of the defense was too far up the field to possibly catch him, but the instant the quarterback threw to the running back, Seth made his move, darting for the ball, leaping for the interception and what would surely be a Falcons' defensive touchdown.

The ball floated in the air. The Packers' runner settled his hips and cupped his arms to catch it. It was all or nothing. If Seth caught it, he would score a touchdown for the Falcons. If he missed, none of the other Falcons' defenders were in position to keep the runner from the end zone.

Seth leaped into the air.

CHAPTER EIGHTEEN

BEFORE SETH'S FINGERTIPS EVEN touched the ball, Troy felt a sickening shift in his gut.

The ball nicked off Seth's fingers.

Seth twisted, landed on one leg, and collapsed.

The Packers' running back adjusted for the tipped ball. It dropped into his arms like bread into a basket. The runner turned and charged ahead. Only a couple of Falcons could even get close, and they were tangled up by plenty of Green Bay blockers. The runner waltzed into the end zone for a touchdown. The hometown crowd booed.

Seth staggered to the sideline. Coach Mora jumped all over him, grabbing hold of the back of Seth's shoulder pad and tagging along with him all the way to the bench.

Troy followed.

"What the heck was *that*?" Mora asked, his face red. "I called a Double Cat Zone so we'd have plenty of backup on that screen, and it looked to me like a dog-gone Cyclone Blitz call. Did you run a Cyclone?"

Seth slumped down on the bench, slammed his helmet on the carpet in front of him, and threw back his head, shaking it with rage. "Yes! I ran a Cyclone, okay? I messed up."

Mora's face contorted with disbelief. Quietly, he asked, "You ran your own play?"

Seth glared at him. "I was trying to make something happen."

Mora barked out a laugh. "You made something happen all right."

"All right," Seth said through clenched teeth. "I messed up. Relax. It's early."

Mora nodded and said, "Okay. Relax. I can do that. But remember this, Halloway. I'm the *coach*. You're the *player*. So, I call the plays. You got that?"

"Okay," Seth said. "Got it."

Mora stomped off. Troy gave Seth a sympathetic look, then shrugged and followed. That wasn't the end of it, though.

The trouble had only begun.

CHAPTER NINETEEN

SETH CALLED COACH MORA'S defenses from that point on, that much was certain. But because of his injured knees and lack of speed, his ability to make the plays a middle linebacker has to make just wasn't there. Once, Seth burst through the line and barreled into the Packers' running back behind the line of scrimmage, but the runner simply stiff-armed him, knocking Seth to the ground. The running back kept going for a twelve-yard gain. Another time, Seth shot untouched around the end of the line on a blitz only to have the quarterback outrun him to the sideline and complete a touchdown pass.

Coach Mora's face darkened from red to purple, and early in the fourth quarter Troy heard him mutter and saw him signal Seth to the sideline.

"That's it," Mora said, meeting Seth as he came off the field. "Your knees are killing you, Seth. I have to make a change."

"Change?"

"Lengyel!" Mora said, barking over his shoulder. "Halloway's down."

"I'm not *down*," Seth said, whipping off his helmet, his words garbled by the mouthpiece he then spit out into his hand. "I can go."

"Not in this game, you can't," Mora said. "We're down by ten. Look at the clock."

Troy glanced up. Only eleven minutes remained in the fourth quarter. Enough time to pull out a win, but not if the Falcons' defense couldn't hold on the next series.

"I can do this," Seth said, sticking out his chin.

"Seth, you know the plays," Mora said, sad and quiet, "and you still can't do it."

"You're better off with me in there and knowing the plays than having Lengyel in there not knowing," Seth said.

"Who says Lengyel won't know?" Mora said. "He's been studying my signals. He can handle it."

"Handle what?" Seth said.

"Me, signaling in the defense and the play they're going to run," Mora said.

The crowded sideline was what Troy imagined a battlefield was like: players rushing back and forth, in and out of the battle depending on its needs. The PAT block team ran out but failed. The kickoff return team surged on, then off the field after a successful return. Then the offense gave a war cry and flooded out. The other Falcons players around them gathered like a silent forest, surrounding Seth, Troy, and Mora, intent on seeing how the conflict would play out.

"If I'm not in there," Seth said, growling through a tight smile and pointing out at the field, "you're not going to know what plays they're running."

"Why?" Mora asked, his face crumpling in confusion.

"Because," Seth said, directing a taped and bloody finger at Troy, "if I'm not in, Troy's not in either."

"Troy?" Mora said. "He works for the team, not you."

"I found Troy," Seth said, nodding to himself. "If it wasn't for me, you wouldn't have him here. We wouldn't be making this run at the playoffs. The whole staff would probably have been fired by now, including you, so don't tell me about Troy working for you."

Coach McFadden, the head coach, pushed his way through the forest of players and into the opening where the action was. Mora explained the situation, and McFadden turned to Troy.

"Well, Troy?" McFadden asked. "Is that true? Are you and Seth a package deal?"

CHAPTER TWENTY

TROY FELT A MIXTURE of anxiety, frustration, and regret.

With everyone now aware of his gift, people expected the Falcons' defense to dominate. He recalled the cameraman's attention before the kickoff and the cheers people in the stands had given him as he walked through the tunnel at halftime. If they lost this important game, he had to believe the enthusiasm all the fans, TV announcers, and agents had shown him would diminish. All the talk about big contracts and other teams bidding for his services would fizzle.

Worst of all, the thrilling little fantasy that had taken hold in his mind—having his dad represent him, the two of them working side by side to come up with some momentous deal—would melt into a soup of confusion.

"Troy," Seth said, breaking through his thoughts, "come on. Tell them."

Troy felt his eyes moisten, but he bit the inside of his lip to pin down his emotions. He knew how much Seth had gone through to get ready to play. Aside from the extensive treatment of ice and heat and the drainage and cortisone shots, Troy remembered the scandal of steroid accusations. Seth had been forced to undergo testing to prove he didn't use the drugs.

Now, after all that, it appeared Seth just couldn't get the job done anyway.

Miserable, Troy looked at the star linebacker and said, "Seth, I can't. They're paying me. My mom says a couple more weeks and I'll have college taken care of."

Troy didn't know which felt worse: the sound of his own simpering excuses or the wounded look on Seth's face before he dropped his head and shuffled over to the bench. Two trainers came forward, got under each of his arms, one on each side, and led him, hobbling now, toward the locker room.

"Thatta boy," Mora said, patting him on the back. "It's football. A team sport. You can't worry about one guy, no matter how much you like him. Come on, Troy, don't look like that. You've got an agreement with the team. When Seth cools down, he'll tell you himself you're doing the right thing. Trust me."

CHAPTER TWENTY-ONE

GRIFFIN LENGYEL WAS BIGGER, faster, and stronger than Seth.

Using Troy's knowledge of the plays, Lengyel looked unstoppable. The defense crushed the Packers. The offense did its part by scoring a pair of touchdowns on passes to Michael Jenkins and Joe Horn. The Falcons ended up winning, 35–31. As the team celebrated, waving their arms to the roaring crowd on their way into the tunnel, Troy's mom put an arm around his shoulder and hugged him tight.

"Mom, I—"

"I know," she said, leaning over and speaking into his ear to cut through the noise, "I heard. Don't worry. You did what you had to. Seth will be okay. I promise. Now listen, I didn't tell you before, but I think you should talk to the press. It'll keep them from hounding us. We can make a decision in a day or two if we want to do any of the shows like *Good Morning America* or *The Tonight Show*, but this will let us knock off all the sports reporters in one shot. I didn't want to say before the game because I know you have to concentrate. You okay with it?"

"Sure."

"It's going to be a little crazy in there," his mom said, "but it'll be better than them following you around and chasing you through the hallways at school."

"They can do that?" Troy asked, his eyes widening.

"Not really," his mom said, "but they will be a pain unless we manage them properly. It starts with you talking at the press conference. There'll be a lot of questions. I'll be there to make sure they don't start asking the same things over and over, and I'll cut it short if you get too uncomfortable. You just tug your ear if you want me to end it. You got that?"

"Sure," Troy said, tugging his ear to show her. "Like this."

"Right," she said, "okay, otherwise, just be honest, and don't be afraid to say you don't know something. They're going to want you to tell them exactly how you do it, but you and I know that's not so easy, so you just do your best. Give them that weather analogy you tell people about how when a cold front and rain head for each other, you can predict snow, and don't worry

if they don't get it. That's their problem. And, if anyone says anything that makes you feel bad, just say to
them 'That's not very nice.' Trust me, coming from a
kid, they'll leave you alone."

"That's not very nice," Troy said to himself, prac-
ticing.

Inside the concrete tunnel, they passed by the locker
room and in through another metal door, where reporters already stood packed in front of a small raised
stage with a podium and a Falcons banner behind it.
The spotlights suspended from a track along the ceiling
blinded Troy temporarily. He shaded his eyes until they
adjusted. His mom spoke into the microphone on top
of the podium, introducing him as the Falcons' "game
management consultant"; that was the official title the
team had come up with, but Troy didn't like it. When
he stepped to the podium and the first question from a
FOX reporter addressed the new title, he remembered
his mom told him just to be honest.

"Game management consultant?" the reporter said.
"Is that what you call yourself?"

"No," Troy said, frowning. "I guess I call myself what
my gramps and my friends call me."

"What's that?"

"Football genius."

The entire place erupted with laughter and clapping. Troy blushed and dipped his head but enjoyed
the response all the same. As his mom predicted,

the reporters couldn't stop asking him how he did it. Finally she stepped in and told them they only had a few more minutes before Coach McFadden would address them.

"What about Seth Halloway?" a reporter from ESPN asked. "You must have been frustrated, giving him the plays and him not being able to make a tackle."

Troy looked at the reporter, then at his mom, who nodded her head. He leaned into the microphone and said, "That's not very nice."

Everyone laughed, and the reporter's face turned cherry.

"Troy," an ABC reporter said, "is it true you're a free agent after this season?"

Troy furrowed his brow.

"Out on the open market," the reporter said. "I heard your agreement with the Falcons is only for this season. Do you have plans afterward to test the open market? And, if so, how much do you think you can get?"

Troy said he wasn't sure and he didn't know.

"You got an agent yet?" another reporter asked.

"No," Troy said, "not yet."

"But you'll get one?"

"Or maybe just a lawyer," Troy said, avoiding his mom's eyes. "Whatever's best."

"Does your deal take the Falcons through the playoffs?" a reporter asked. "Do you have a bonus if you help them win the Super Bowl?"

Troy looked at his mom and tugged his ear. She stepped back to the podium, leaning over his shoulder, and said, "Troy is set through the season with the Falcons, however far it takes them. Okay, thank you all; we've got Coach McFadden coming in now."

The concrete room exploded with questions from all sides. Troy's mom took Troy by the arm and led him down the small flight of steps and out the side door, leaving the storm of shouting and confusion behind. Coach McFadden brushed past with Troy's mom's boss, Cecilia Fetters, and gave Troy a pat on the shoulder.

"Heck of a job out there today, son," the coach said before disappearing through the door.

Troy followed his mom down the relatively quiet tunnel. Only some police officers stood outside the locker room, while a small stream of stadium workers, cheerleaders, and Falcons employees flowed past. Nathan and Tate sat on a golf cart, waiting with grins over all the up-close excitement.

"Everyone ready?" Troy's mom asked.

"Don't you have more work?" Troy asked, knowing that his mom typically couldn't leave the stadium until the last of the players had gone.

"I'm on a new assignment," she said, running her hand over the back of his head and sending a chill down his back. "You."

"You work for Troy now?" Nathan said. Somewhere he'd found a box of popcorn, and as he asked the question, a piece of popcorn escaped his mouth.

"Don't get carried away," Troy's mom said. "Mr. Langan just doesn't want him getting cornered by some reporter somewhere without backup. That's me."

As they turned to go, Seth emerged from the locker room door, already showered and in his street clothes of jeans and a button-down shirt. Both his knees had been packed and wrapped in ice. When he saw them, he pulled up short. His eyes were sunken with exhaustion and pain.

"Troy," Seth said, his voice raspy with emotion. "Can I talk to you?"

"Sure," Troy said, looking down and waiting for a scolding.

Seth said, "I mean, alone."

CHAPTER TWENTY-TWO

TROY LOOKED UP AT his mom. She inclined her head toward Seth, signaling for Troy to go. Troy followed Seth down the concrete hallway for a bit, stopping in a quiet corner where two metal doors opened into another section. Seth turned to face Troy, his long dark hair still wet from the shower. His face—Troy saw now— was drawn not only from pain and exhaustion but from sadness. Troy jammed his left hand into his pocket and clutched his father's business card. Somehow, it gave him comfort.

"Hey," Seth said, the word without tone or meaning.

"Seth, I'm sorry," Troy said, blurting out his apology.

Seth grimaced and held up a hand for Troy to stop. "Please. I'm the one who's sorry. How I acted out there, well, it wasn't fair to you."

"Seth," Troy said, "you're right, though. Without you, none of this would have happened. The Falcons never would have given me a chance. Without you, Tate and Nathan and I wouldn't be champs. Our team never could have gotten into the junior league playoffs, let alone win the whole thing."

"But I didn't coach the team because I wanted you to help me with the plays," Seth said. "I mean, I wanted you to help me, but that's not why I coached you guys. I had fun. I like you, Troy, *and* Nathan and Tate. And I love your mom. I wanted to help just to help, and I had a heck of a lot of fun doing it."

"Even with all the rumors in the newspaper?" Troy said, thinking of the scandal and the damage to Seth's reputation when the paper and others in the media falsely accused him of being a steroid user.

"Yeah," Seth said. "Even with that. Good things don't usually come easy, you know. There's almost always a price."

"Gramps said something like that to me just yesterday," Troy said, releasing the card to motion excitedly. "He said, 'Anything worth having is worth fighting for.'"

"See?" Seth said. "Great minds think alike. So, yeah, it was worth it, even with the trouble. And you and I are okay now. With this. You've got an incredible gift, and I don't want anyone to ruin it for you, especially me. I want you to use it and have fun and make all the money you can. Buy that house for you and your mom.

Get her that Benz we talked about. And I don't want you worrying about me, because I'll be fine."

"Are you mad at the Falcons?" Troy asked.

"Nah," Seth said, "it's business, this NFL thing. They've got to win or they're gone, too. It's just how it is. But if that's the way they're going to play it, then you get yourself the best doggone agent out there and hammer them on a long-term deal, okay? I can have my agent give you a call if you want. John Marchiano. The guy is honest and good. That's what you need."

"Well," Troy said, thinking of his father and the card in his pocket. "Maybe. I was thinking of getting a lawyer instead."

Seth pulled his head back and gave Troy a curious look. "How about you? Talking agents and lawyers."

"Just an idea," Troy said, shrugging.

"Well, Marchiano is a lawyer, too, so you're all set."

"Maybe," Troy said, wavering.

"Well, whatever you and your mom decide," Seth said. "Not my business, really."

"Is this it for you, Seth?" Troy asked, his eyes wandering down to the ice bags packed to either side of both knees.

"I'm not going to say that," Seth said, shifting his weight from one bad leg to the other with discomfort. "Today, well, I didn't have it, but I've seen guys come back, get better. They're not usually my age, but it can happen."

"So, you want to keep playing?" Troy asked.

Seth heaved a long, tired sigh but nodded his head slowly as he released his breath. "I do. I know a few days ago I said I was tired and sore and all that, but being pulled from that game today? That made me realize how much I want to keep doing it. So, I'll get to work on these bad joints and see if I can't get the swelling down enough to get back into running shape. If not this week then the next, or the week after that. The way we're going with you, it looks like we're headed for the play-offs, so I'm not going to give up until the day after the Super Bowl, because if we're in it and there's any way at all I can play, you better believe I'll be there. Even if it's just to block on the punt team."

Seth smiled at him, and for a moment it outshone his weariness. Then the spark went out. Troy felt an ache in his chest for the man who he could only dream of getting an autograph from a few months ago.

"I get that," Troy said. "Seth?"

"Yeah?"

"What about this Border War game?" Troy asked. "Do you think you'll still be able to coach that?"

Seth smiled painfully and said, "Funny thing about me is that when I say I'll do something, I never back out. Plus, if my career *is* over, it won't hurt me to have the top coaches in the SEC see *me* in action either. You never know where your first break in that business is going to come. Yeah, I'm coaching. And you're playing, right? Even though you're in the big time now with an agent or a lawyer or whatever?"

"Sure I'm playing," Troy said. "I'd love to go to Georgia, and like you said, those coaches will be watching, so . . ."

"Okay, good," Seth said, shuffling toward the door. "Now, I'm headed home."

"I thought my mom was going to pick up some ribs from Fat Matt's and we were going to watch the Sunday night game?" Troy said.

Seth let out a sharp, bitter laugh. "I've had enough football for one day. Tell your mom thanks, and I'll call her later."

"Won't she be kind of mad?" Troy asked, glancing over his shoulder at where his mom now stood talking to her boss.

"Not her," Seth said. "That's one of the reasons I love her. She doesn't get bent out of shape about little things like that. She knows how I get about being hurt. I'm not good company right now. Besides, I need to just get home and get to work on these knees."

Seth reached into the front pocket of his jeans and removed a pill bottle that he shook gently at Troy. "I've got some heavy-duty medicine and an appointment with a bucket of ice in my tub. Speaking of ice, you'd better stick your finger in some, too."

"Medicine? Like painkillers?" Troy asked, his forehead crunching up with concern.

"No," Seth said, stuffing the amber plastic bottle into his pocket and beginning to walk away again, "an anti-inflammatory. Same stuff they give to racehorses."

Troy's jaw went slack, but before he could say anything else, Seth had disappeared. He sensed Tate at his side and turned to see that his mom and Nathan were also there.

"How is he?" Troy's mom asked, her eyes following the arc of the metal door as it swung closed. "Was he mad?"

"He said he'd call you later, Mom," Troy said. "Mad? No, he wasn't mad. I'd say more like hurt."

"Mentally?" his mom asked. "Or physically?"

Troy looked at his mom. "I'd have to say both."

CHAPTER TWENTY-THREE

AS SETH PREDICTED, TROY'S mom did understand when Troy explained what Seth had said about not being good company and wanting to get started on icing his knees. She still stopped at Fat Matt's, and they ate ribs and grilled chicken back at Troy's house, watching the beginning of *Sunday Night Football*. Between eating, Troy's left hand kept secretly returning to his pocket to caress the corners of his father's business card while his right hand stayed dipped in a big glass that held icy water for his hurt finger. Normally, he would have wanted Tate and Nathan to stay as long as they could, but he was relieved when Tate licked the BBQ sauce from her fingers and stood to go.

Troy saw them to the door, and Tate and Nathan disappeared into the pines, headed down to the tracks that would take them home. As soon as his friends had left, Troy removed his father's card from his pocket, studied it, then put it back. He marched into the living room. The Styrofoam boxes from Fat Matt's still lay about the coffee table, but his mom had already disappeared into her bedroom. He could hear her talking to Seth on the phone. Troy tried to ignore the soft, gooey sound of her voice through the door as she offered sympathy and comfort to the star linebacker.

Troy turned off the TV in the living room and waited impatiently. Finally, he heard his mom tell Seth that she loved him, and her bedroom door creaked open.

"What?" she asked. "You're not watching the game? You feeling okay?"

"I want to call my dad," Troy said, his hand sneaking back into his pocket to clench the rumpled card.

His mom sighed, then her face did that thing where her chin went up and the corners of her mouth tugged out and down into little crescent-shaped wrinkles. "Yes, we need to talk about that."

"I want to see him," Troy said, "and you said that if he tried to sue for me, you'd let me see him. You said. Gramps was right here."

"Right," she said, drawing out the word. "He's suing me. Funny how that happened all of a sudden at the dome, after you spoke with him."

"He came up to me," Troy said, feeling the ground slip out from under him. His stomach sank, because he knew where this was headed and he knew his mom couldn't be fooled. Even so, he had to try. "Gramps said my dad needed to prove I wasn't just a whim because he saw me on *Larry King*, and he asked his client to get him passes so he could see me. That proves it wasn't just a whim."

His mom looked at him for a long moment before she put her hands on her hips and said, "But it wasn't his idea, the lawsuit thing, was it?"

Troy's mind went into hyperdrive. "He's a lawyer, Mom. You heard him. He knows all about that stuff."

A grim smile lit his mom's lips. "You didn't answer my question and I'm glad you didn't, because I think it means you respect me enough not to lie. Now, I know, and you know, that Drew didn't think up that lawsuit business. You just kind of mentioned it to him, didn't you?"

"He came to the game because of me," Troy said, panic filling him.

"But that's not the same thing," she said. "That's not what we agreed to."

Troy's sweaty hand dampened the card. The pressure in his head felt like a boiling pot, and his hurt finger throbbed. He tried to contain his rage, but it burst, and he yelled, "That's my father, and I want to see him! I *will* see him!"

His mom's voice went eerily calm. "No, you won't see him unless I say you'll see him. I'm keeping that number. Now, I'll live up to my original agreement. *If* he really sues me, then we'll work something out, but no more coaching from you."

"He said he was going to!" Troy said, banging his good hand on the coffee table so that a container of chewed-over rib bones spilled to the floor, making a mess.

"He's said a lot of things in his day," she said bitterly. "You don't have any idea, Troy."

His mom marched into the kitchen, and he heard her rattling something. Troy got up and followed to see her removing the phone from the wall. She marched back out into the living room and pointed at the mess.

"Clean that up and then get to bed," she said. "You've got school in the morning. You can take another pill for your finger if you need it."

"What are you doing with the phone?" he asked.

"It'll be with me, along with my cell phone," she said, starting toward her bedroom before stopping in the hallway and spinning around. "It's not that I don't love you, Troy, but I can't say one hundred percent that I trust you. I know how you get, and I can see that look in your eye. I don't want you searching the internet all night, finding his number, and calling him. I'll keep the phone with me to make it easier for you to do what I'm telling you to do. Now, good night."

"But he's leaving tomorrow night," Troy said, his voice barely a whisper.

His mom disappeared without another word, gently closing her door with a final click.

Troy's muscles tightened until he shook. He picked up a pillow and whacked it against the arm of the couch until dust glimmered in yellow light from the lamp next to his mom's La-Z-Boy. He sneezed and huffed and threw down the pillow before slumping to the floor and holding his head in his hands, crying and growling to himself with rage.

Finally, he took a deep, ragged breath, cleaned up, and went to bed.

He hadn't lain there for more than ten minutes before he sprang from his bed, dressed, and slipped out the window into the night.

If he couldn't call his father, Troy had a different and better idea of how he could see him, and he wouldn't have to wait.

CHAPTER TWENTY-FOUR

THE TREES ABOVE SHIFTED restlessly in a steady wind that smelled like coming rain, and stars blinked between tattered holes in the clouds. Behind the toolshed lay his gramps's fourteen-foot aluminum ladder, and Troy knew he could lift it on his own. He found the middle two rungs and picked up the ladder, bumping his finger and cursing to himself. Struggling, he poked his head through so the ladder rested on his shoulders like a bizarre collar that balanced nicely. He knew the way through the dark pinewoods to the railroad bed almost without looking. The dull glow of the tracks lay like discarded stilts, pointing the way to where his friends lived and making him wish they were with him. He stood for a moment, thinking, then decided it would take too long to get them, even if they could sneak away.

Besides, this was something he needed to do on his own.

This was a family thing.

He stepped carefully through the weeds onto a once-familiar path now overgrown and filled with ruts and gopher holes. Through the trees, he navigated the big ladder, his eyes recognizing the dull gray lines of the concrete wall like an old enemy's face in a crowd. It surrounded the entire Cotton Wood Country Club. He spotted his old way in—a gaping crack—that had since been patched with concrete and cobblestones. Troy raised the ladder off his shoulders, breathing with deep relief at the lifted weight. He braced the ladder against the wall, scaling it quickly.

Nearly a foot thick, the wall provided an ample perch for him at its top. He stood and stared, listening for any sign of life from within, but the wind cloaked all other sounds. He wiggled his feet, setting them firm, and lowered his center before raising the ladder up and over to the other side. After planting it in the dirt below, he swung out and around and climbed down. Because he'd been inside the country club so many times before—as an intruder, but more recently as Seth's guest—he knew well the way he had to go.

Even so, he kept to the shadows, avoiding the glow of street lamps and hustling along with his feet swishing through the grass shoulders of the quiet streets. The maze of winding roads and mansions nestled back in the trees or on hilltops behind iron or brick fences led him to an enormous home on the biggest hill in Cotton Wood. With lights shining up from the bushes and grass, the huge white building looked more like a museum or an old government statehouse than one man's home. The stone wall that ran along the street was for decoration, not defense, and Troy scaled it with ease. He snuck through the bushes up along a curved driveway until he came to a courtyard with a hissing fountain in its center. The driveway was crowded with glossy cars whose glittering grillwork reminded Troy of the rap star's own teeth.

Amid the Bentley, Mercedes, and Lexus vehicles—all midnight blue or black—Troy spotted the orange Porsche his father had driven into Seth's driveway. His heart pattered, but he wasn't certain if that was because he knew his father was inside or because of the men in dark suits with walkie-talkies he now saw prowling the perimeter of the house. Troy looked down at his own gray hooded sweatshirt and simple white V-neck T-shirt with faded jeans and sneakers. He sighed and popped out of the shrubbery, heading up the stone walkway for the broad front steps. A man in a suit stepped out from behind one of the tall, fluted columns. He met Troy halfway up, arresting his progress with an iron hand. He spoke softly but urgently into his walkie-talkie about a kid appearing out of nowhere.

CHAPTER TWENTY-FIVE

"YOU LOST, KID?" THE security guard asked, scowling.

"I'm looking for my father," Troy said. "Drew Edinger. He's G Money's lawyer. That's his car."

The guard looked over at the orange Porsche and raised his eyebrows, retelling Troy's story into the radio.

The radio scratched the air, then a raspy voice said, "Bring him back to the pool."

The guard angled his head for Troy to follow him up onto the porch, through the massive front doors, and into a foyer that rose three stories. A curved stairway opened off to the left, and a fifteen-foot painting of G Money in a red three-piece suit with a fur hat tow-ered over them on the curved wall to the right. Troy looked up at a glittering chandelier. The domed ceiling above was painted like a blue sky with puffy clouds and angels.

"Wow," Troy heard himself say as they passed a suit of armor and entered another enormous room, filled with furniture upholstered in the skins of zoo animals: zebras, leopards, lions, and bears. They walked through some glass doors and into the back, where the wings on either side of the house flanked a pool. It was like nothing Troy had ever seen. Instead of an aqua blue bottom with stone or wood decking, this pool's bottom was midnight blue with tiny glimmering stars. It looked as if you'd be jumping into space. The pool's rounded triangular shape made it seem to Troy as if he were standing on the deck of a spaceship from some Star Wars movie.

So fascinated was Troy by the pool that he bumped into the guard, who had stopped at the foot of a stone terrace. A handful of men sat around a circular table playing cards, drinking colorful drinks in tall, clear glasses. Most of them wore sparkling chains, rings, and sunglasses, even though it was dark. The night closed in around them, and the low lights surrounding the terrace and pool did little to battle it back. Strangely, the music that wafted up from hidden speakers was the furthest thing from G Money's rap that Troy could imagine. This music was calm and soothing: wood flutes, synthesizers, and the sounds of trickling water.

Troy's father stood up from the table. He wore only a

button-down shirt, suit pants, and his diamond watch. He removed a cigar from his mouth, blowing a plume of blue smoke into the air before enthusiastically introducing Troy around the table. Men with more tattoos, scars, and gold than Troy had ever seen glanced up to briefly say hello. One of them was the enormous bald man with the cold blue eyes Troy had seen in the dome. G Money called them his homeys, and since the men were dressed in colorful silk, leather, and suede, Troy felt silly in his sweatshirt and jeans. He looked down and swatted at the smudge marks on his shirt before running a hand through his hair and shaking his father's hand. His father pulled him close and hugged him tight, patting Troy's back.

"Hey, Drew," said a short, fat man with a crooked Celtics hat and a face as round as a basketball, "that's your big-time ticket, right? The kid?"

Drew scowled at the man and looked to G Money, but it was the man with the bald pink head, rimless rectangular glasses, and a jaguar's head tattooed up the side of his neck who spoke.

"Bubbles, you're always talking," the big man said, his voice rumbling like a volcano ready to blow and flashes of gold teeth appearing from the midst of his furry black beard. "I need to put a rat trap on your chin and then maybe you'd keep that tongue inside your head."

The entire table went quiet, and Troy knew that

each one of the men was afraid of the big man, even G Money. Drew quietly excused himself to G Money and nodded at the big man. Then he led Troy down some side steps to a swinging bench seat. Heat lamps on the terrace warmed them against the cool fall night.

"Ticket?" Troy asked.

Drew waved his hand dismissively and said, "Bubbles washes the cars. He's a moron."

"Who's that big scary-looking guy?" Troy asked.

"Just a friend of G Money's from Chicago," Drew said. "He helped G Money get started in the business. His name is Luther Tolsky. He knows a lot of people."

Troy nodded, then quietly said, "Weird music."

"G Money is into Zen," Drew said.

"Like, the religion?"

"He says it helps his rap to be pure," Drew said, scowling at his cigar and butting it out against the lip of a large clay pot containing a lemon tree. "Have a seat. Where's your mom?"

Troy folded his hands in his lap and studied them before he said, "Home."

"At Seth Halloway's?" Drew asked.

"No. We live just outside the wall," Troy said, pointing in the general direction of their house.

"Wall?"

"There's a wall around the club," Troy said. "We live in the pinewoods just outside. It's nice. I got a tire to throw footballs through."

"And she's there?" his father asked.

Troy nodded.

"But, how'd you get *here*?" his father asked.

Troy waved his hand toward where he'd scaled the wall and said, "Just walked. I knew where G Money's house was."

Drew looked at his watch, then at Troy, and asked, "And she's okay with this? Walked, as in climbed-the-wall walked? Or you walked all the way around? Wait, don't answer that. I don't want to know."

Troy's mouth fell open.

"Troy," his father said, leaning toward him with all of the friendliness draining from his face, "don't even tell me that your mom doesn't know you're here."

"Why?" Troy said, laughing nervously. "It's no big deal."

His father shook his head and said, "Oh, yes it is."

CHAPTER TWENTY-SIX

"BUT," TROY SAID, HIS voice barely rising above the muted chatter of the nearby cardplayers, "you said you wanted to see me."

"And I do," his father said, nodding his head, "but not like this, not sneaking around. No, wait. Don't drop your head like that. You didn't do anything wrong. It's just that I don't want her to ruin it. If we give her an excuse to act out—any excuse—she'll use it. There are reasons I didn't stay with her, Troy, and none of it had anything to do with you. Like I said, I didn't even know about you."

Troy studied his father's face: the brown eyes flecked with shards as black as tar. They whirled like hypnotic tops. Troy thought of the annoying things his mom could do, the way she managed him like a circus tiger:

cutting him off; making him sit, roll over, and jump through hoops of fire. She claimed it was all for his own good, but he knew how any little deviation from the rules, any misstep, led to consequences that were always severe.

"I know what you mean," Troy said.

His father put a hand on Troy's shoulder and squeezed. "So, here's what we do. We get you back before she knows you're gone, and then we do this thing right."

"But you're leaving tomorrow," Troy said.

His father's grin reappeared, and he tilted his head. "I was supposed to, but if you think I'm leaving without getting this straightened out, you've got another think coming. Troy, do you realize how excited I am to have a son? Forget about how great a football player you are and this football genius thing. I've always wanted someone to go hunting and fishing and to ball games with—all that stuff."

Troy felt his heart swell.

"Come on," his dad said, rising from their seat, "let me drive you home. I can let you off on the street, where she won't even see us together."

Troy shook his head and said, "Honestly, it's better for me to just go back the way I came. Once I get over the wall, it's a shorter walk than if you let me off at the top of my driveway."

"Whatever works," his father said.

"You could help me out, if you don't mind," Troy said. "Maybe drive me to the back of the development. If you're with me, I won't have to worry about the security guards."

"Guards? You mean G Money's guards?" his father asked.

"No, the Cotton Wood guards," Troy said.

His father raised his eyebrows. They stopped to say good-bye to G Money, and the rapper told Troy's dad to hurry because he wanted to win back his money. Troy climbed into the front seat of the Porsche next to his father. The smooth leather and green, glowing numbers on the control panel reminded him of a space rocket and G Money's pool.

"Is this yours?" Troy asked.

His father grinned and nodded as he fired up the engine. "Brought it down from Chicago. I was itching for a road trip. Clears my head to drive a thousand miles in a machine like this."

Troy nodded.

"That's some pool he's got," Troy said, pointing out the way his father should go.

"A million bucks, just for the pool alone," his father said, glancing at him. "Twelve for the house."

"Up there," Troy said, pointing to a maintenance road that led to a shed back behind part of the golf course.

His dad pulled the Porsche up the gravel path

through the trees and stopped in the dusty lot beside the massive shed. Tractors, golf carts, and other odd-shaped machinery lurked in the shadows cast by a single light mounted on the shed wall. Dust settled in the headlights' beams, and his father shut off the engine. Trees whispered above.

"What are you doing?" Troy asked.

"How about I go with you?" his father said.

"Over the wall?"

"I'd like to see where you live," he said, "make sure you get back safe."

"I have to take the ladder with me," Troy said, warmed, though, by the thought of his father wanting to do something dangerous and outside the lines with him.

"It's not far, right?" Drew said.

"No."

"So, you can show me, then bring me back and take the ladder with you."

Troy hesitated and bit his lower lip.

"You don't have to," Drew said.

"No, it's not that," Troy said. "I was thinking, maybe I could show you the bridge."

"Bridge?"

"The railroad tracks are back there, and there's a bridge not too far down that crosses the Hooch—the Chattahoochee River," Troy said. "I like to go there sometimes, to think."

"Like a special place?" his father asked.

Troy nodded.

"So, show me the way," his father said. "I'd love to see it. I'd be honored."

Excitement bloomed in Troy's chest. He got out of the shiny orange car, slamming the door and trying not to run for the wall. He turned to see his father taking long strides to catch up. When they reached the wall, Troy went to the left. His gramps's ladder lay tucked into the underbrush about fifty feet away. He crouched and raised it up, his father helping to brace it against the wall.

"Feel like I'm twelve myself," his father said under his breath as he steadied the ladder and Troy climbed up.

When he reached the top, Troy said, "Now you come up, then we'll pull the ladder over."

It took several minutes, but soon Troy was leading his father down the tracks toward the steel trestle spanning the river. He had so many questions—questions that had haunted him for years—and now, finally, it looked as if he might have the chance to get the answers.

CHAPTER TWENTY-SEVEN

TROY SHOWED HIS FATHER how he and Tate sat, with legs dangling in space. The river below slogged along, reflecting the ghostly tatters of clouds above as they swept across the starry sky.

"Nice spot to think," his father said, swinging his legs and bracing his arms against the metal beam above so he could lean out over the empty space.

"Can I ask you some questions?" Troy asked.

"Shoot."

"Do you have any other kids? Do I have a brother or sister or anything?" Troy asked.

"Nope," Drew said. "I was married for a bit, but that didn't work out, and we never had kids. She was too busy. That's why it never worked. My own parents are gone, and the one sister I had died in a car accident about a year ago. So, it's just me. That makes finding you even more special."

"And you live in Chicago, right?" Troy asked.

"Got a condo in Lake Point Tower," his father said.

Troy gave him a confused look.

"It's the top place in Chicago," his father explained. "Downtown high-rise, right on the lake. I can walk to my law office. You'll come see it."

"There's a train that Tate calls the Midnight Express," Troy said, pointing to the other side of the trestle and the tracks that extended as far as they could see. "Atlanta to Chicago. I hear it sometimes at night and I'd always think of you, even though I didn't know you."

His father seemed to consider the northbound tracks but didn't say anything.

"And you played football, right?" Troy said.

"Pretty well, too," his father said with a chuckle, "until I broke my neck. Oh, it wasn't that bad. I got lucky, actually. They said another eighth of an inch and I wouldn't be walking. They fused two vertebrae together, and it healed pretty good—but not in time for anything in the pros. I missed my train, so to speak. A lot of people do."

"That's what I want to do," Troy said. "Make it to the NFL."

"Maybe you will," his father said. "I'm actually in the Auburn record books myself, so you got the genes, the speed, the athleticism. Now all you need is a little luck. Tell me about this genius thing."

"My gramps told me you were a math major," Troy said. "Kind of weird for a football player. I was wondering if you can kind of do what I can do. I can't really explain it, but Seth says it's about probabilities based on the variables in the game. That sounds like math to me."

His father turned his head and studied Troy's face in the dim light. "Seth, huh?"

"He's been pretty good to me," Troy said.

"Like a father?"

"No, more like a friend," Troy said.

"Good," Drew said, his teeth showing in his smile. "It's funny you said that about how you can't really explain it. That's how math was for me. I really wasn't big when it came to school. I never really applied myself until law school. But I could take these advanced math classes and just . . . know it. I didn't even really like math. It all just made sense to me: the formulas, the theorems, the way numbers can predict not just lines but curves, even waves, even across three dimensions. Are you good in math?"

"Nope," Troy said. "My mom says I'm a savant. Pretty normal except when it comes to football. That's why they say 'football genius.'"

"A prodigious savant," his father said as if to himself.

"What?" Troy asked.

"Not a savant, really," his father said, reaching out and putting a strong hand on Troy's shoulder. "I mean, you are, but you're more. It's savant syndrome, and almost everyone who has it also has a developmental disability—autism lots of times—except for one narrow area where they're so smart, they're off the charts. A prodigious savant is extremely rare. That's a person who's normal in every other way—no disability, no brain injury, nothing; just a prodigy. 'Genius' is a good name for it—in some narrow area. Wow."

"And it's a good thing, right?" Troy asked.

"Ha!" his father said, shaking his head. "Good? It's great. Look at you: a normal kid, but you can predict plays in an NFL game? Troy, my biggest concern is that no one takes advantage of you."

"Who'd do that?" Troy asked.

His father sighed and shook his head, the wind ruffling his shaggy brown hair, the strong bones in his face carving out shadows even in the weak starlight. "The world is a vicious place, Troy. Trust me. The things I've seen."

"But you can help me, right?" Troy asked. "I mean, you want to, right?"

His father tightened the grip on Troy's shoulder and

said, "Of course I want to, and I'm the perfect person to do it, with everything I've seen, knowing sports, knowing the entertainment industry.

"But there's just one problem."

CHAPTER TWENTY-EIGHT

"**I DOUBT YOUR MOTHER** will let me help," Drew said.

"Why wouldn't she?" Troy asked, searching his father's face in the shadows.

"You see the way she thinks of me," Drew said. "It's hard for people to blame themselves, and anyway, I'm sure Seth Halloway is going to push you to use his agent."

"He actually mentioned it already," Troy said under his breath.

"See?" Drew said. "That's how these things work. Clients know if they do their agent a favor, they get a favor back. That's one of the things I'm worried about for you. You don't know how long this is going to last, and you need a long-term deal that gets you the most you can possibly get."

"What do you mean, 'last'?" Troy asked.

"You see patterns that let you predict the outcome," his father said. "The way I see it, it's all about tendencies. Well, people can break tendencies. Go against the pattern."

Troy thought for a minute, then said, "But if they go against one pattern, wouldn't that just make another pattern?"

"In theory," Drew said. "But what if they just randomize the play calling?"

"Well," Troy said, "they might end up running a quarterback sneak on third and twelve. That wouldn't make sense, right?"

"I understand that," Drew said. "Look, I don't know all the possibilities. I'm just saying that, right now, you're worth a lot of money, and I'd like to make sure that you get it. I don't want to see you pawned off to some agent just because he knows Seth Halloway."

"Well, Seth's not my dad. He's my friend, but not my dad. Why can't you just do the deal for me?" Troy said, his heart galloping now. "You're a lawyer, and lawyers are even better than agents, right?"

"Believe me, I'd love to," Drew said.

"Great," Troy said. "Perfect."

"I'm telling you, Troy," Drew said, shaking his head. "She's not going to go for it. If I am going to help, we'll have to be smart about it."

"We can do that," Troy said. "You file the papers you

need to tomorrow and then she has to let me see you. That's the deal."

"I thought you said if I told her I'd sue her she'd let you see me," Drew said.

"Well," Troy said, "she kind of figured out that I tipped you off. She wants to make sure you follow through."

"That's easy," Drew said. "I can draw up the papers in the morning."

"Then I can tell her that I want you to do the deal for me," Troy said, his voice rising up toward the stars. "She can't say no. It's my deal. I'm the football genius, right? What do you think?"

"I think that if we're going to have a chance," his father said, patting Troy's shoulder and then standing up, "then we'd better get you back. I like your plan. It's smart. So, let's not give her an excuse to stop us before we even get started."

They walked back down the tracks, and Troy assured his father he could get the ladder back on his own. Troy watched him climb up to the top of the wall and give him a salute before crouching down and lowering himself over the other side. Troy heard his father drop to the earth with a thud, and he flattened his hands against the cool concrete wall, sad to be alone.

"You okay?" he asked, shouting so his voice would carry up and over the wall.

"Yeah," his father said, sounding far away. "I'll see you soon."

"Tomorrow," Troy said, nodding to himself.

"Don't worry," Troy's father said, his voice moving away, "I'm not going anywhere."

Troy grabbed the ladder. He lowered it slowly, then balanced it on his shoulders. By the time he dumped the ladder down behind the shed, he'd worked up a sweat. Using a thick piece of firewood as a step, he climbed inside through his bedroom window. After removing his sweaty clothes, Troy lay panting in his underwear. The wind in the pines and the dull thump of his own heartbeat did nothing to help him sleep.

He thought of all the important things that had happened to him in the past few months: the excitement of working for the Atlanta Falcons, winning a state championship, appearing on TV, the money he'd made already, and the huge money he was about to make. None of it compared to tomorrow, though. The thought of having his own father be an official part of his life—spending time together, taking trips, throwing a football, or even just talking—made everything else seem like Halloween candy compared to a Christmas present. The other stuff was good and seemed really exciting when he got it, but this was something deep. This was something he'd dreamed about so hard for so long that he felt something had shifted in his core.

The change was so dramatic that the very world around him seemed a different place.

The only problem was that, despite his father's words

of assurance and despite the deal he had with his mom, something gnawed at him, telling him that nothing was for sure. Maybe it was his mom's own doubts about his dad. She hadn't been shy about showing her dislike and even her contempt for him.

Troy sighed and rolled over in the sheets, knowing that if sleep came, it wouldn't come easy.

Everything hinged on tomorrow.

CHAPTER TWENTY-NINE

TROY LAY COMFORTABLY IN his dream on a sandy beach with the wind slipping past. He knew it was a dream, and he didn't want to wake up, despite the sound of his mom's insistent voice. Finally, when he knew for certain she wasn't going away, Troy opened his eyes and realized that his finger felt better even though it was swollen and stiff.

"Wake up," she said again. "I let you sleep late."

"You did?" Troy asked, swinging his legs out of bed.

"Home Economics first period, right?" she said. "I'm sorry, but learning to bake a cake from a box when the kids in this country rank twenty-fourth in the world in math scores? That's ridiculous."

Troy grinned but felt a pang of guilt for plotting with

his father to trick a mom cool enough to let him skip Home Ec.

"What? You like cake from a box?" she asked.

"No, I'm glad," he said. "I was just thinking about everything."

"Your father?" she said with a sigh. "I know. Come on, I made oatmeal."

"Everything else, too," he said, following her into the hallway. "The TV shows. A big contract. The agents."

"I've been thinking about that," she said. "The TV shows aren't going to go away. I think we get the agent thing worked out first. Whoever we choose will probably have some specific ideas on how we can work this to our best advantage. We need to use the media in this to help our negotiations. We need to get you the best deal we can, Troy. This is serious business."

Troy followed her into the kitchen in his boxer shorts. At the stove, she took a metal spoon and began stirring a pot of oatmeal with vicious intensity. He was dying to tell her that she and his father were now thinking along the exact same lines, but for some unknown reason the harsh, scraping sound made him hold his tongue.

"What are you doing?" she asked, turning to dollop out the oatmeal into the pair of bowls she'd put on the table but stopping to stare. "Get dressed. It's going to be beautiful today, so you can wear shorts if you want. What, Troy? You're acting strange."

Troy forced a smile and shook his head before scooting back down the hall to use the bathroom and dress. He sat down to a steaming bowl of oatmeal with raisins and banana slices and dug in.

When his mom dropped him off at school, she signed him in at the office. He hugged her tight before heading for his locker. He was in the hallway outside math class when Tate found him and asked where he'd been. Troy explained about his mom letting him sleep in before launching proudly into the newfound information he had on his father. Nathan joined them halfway through Troy's glowing report. When he'd finished, Nathan whistled low.

"Records at Auburn," Nathan said. "That's sweet."

"Wow. Who else does he represent besides G Money?" Tate asked.

"I don't know," Troy said, his excitement riding high. He began to tell them the story of the night before—sneaking out, G Money's mansion, and his dad climbing the wall with him—but the bell rang before he could finish, and his friends had to stay in suspense until third-period study hall, when they all got library passes.

Troy got on the computer and, armed with his father's name, Googled the former college star turned big-time lawyer, proudly pulling up the Auburn University football record book.

"Look," he said, pointing out his dad's name in the

record books, once for being third in total rushing yards in a season and another for tying for first with five touchdowns in a single game.

"The real deal," Nathan said quietly.

"That's great, Troy," Tate said.

Troy looked up and in a hushed library voice finished telling them the story about the night before. When he stopped talking, Troy noticed that Tate was gnawing gently on her knuckle.

"What's wrong?" Troy asked.

Tate hesitated, then said, "You don't really think you can fool your mom, do you?"

"I'm not 'fooling' her, Tate," he said. "I'm just . . . I don't know, playing out the situation."

"Right," she said, "manipulating."

"Don't even listen to her," Nathan said, swatting the air. "It's a great plan. Your mom will be happy, and you'll get a big-time contract *and* your dad back all at once. It's perfect. I'm happy for you, Troy. Can't you just be happy for the man, Tate?"

Tate scowled at Nathan, raised her voice, and said, "Telling someone what they want to hear might be your idea of being a friend, but it's not mine. I don't like it, that's all. I'm just telling him how I feel."

Tate looked at Troy and Nathan, obviously wondering if they'd be heading back to study hall with her, but Nathan scooted his chair closer to the computer screen and put an arm around Troy's shoulder.

"Come on, Troy," he said in a whisper, "let's Google his clients and see who else he reps besides you and G Money."

Tate nodded for Troy to go ahead, then walked away. Troy turned eagerly back toward the screen, thrilled at the prospect of what he might find. G Money was as big as it got, though. The rest of his dad's clients—at least the ones he could locate from newspaper articles and websites—were names he had only remotely heard of, if at all.

"Hey, what's that?" Nathan asked, still hungry for more names he recognized. "Northlake Trust? That's a band, right?"

Troy's fingers danced over the keys as he refined his search.

"It's my dad's client, but it's no band," he said, reading. "In fact, whoever they are, it looks like they're in some pretty big trouble."

CHAPTER THIRTY

TROY LEANED TOWARD THE screen, afraid that what he saw might somehow affect his mom's outlook on Troy reuniting with his dad.

"Stuff here with the IRS and the Justice Department?" Troy said, trying to talk lightly. "Man, I guess sometimes being a lawyer is going to get you mixed up with some suspicious characters."

"So long as their money's green, right?" Nathan said.

When Troy looked at him, Nathan shrugged and said, "Hey, I saw it on TV."

"Well," Troy said, glancing at the clock. "Enough for now. I'm sure there are some other big-time people he keeps under wraps, you know, confidentiality and all that. A lawyer has to know how to keep quiet."

121

"Yeah, that's for sure," Nathan said. "Everyone knows that."

At lunch, the talk about Troy's dad continued. Only a couple of times during the day did the three friends discuss the Border War game, but when they did Troy assured them both that his finger was so much better that he thought he might even be able to practice the next night if he taped it up tight.

"Awesome," Tate said. "That scholarship money's got my name on it."

"You and me both, sister," Nathan said, slurping the last bit of milk from his carton with a straw. "My cousin says you can't go to college without a flat-screen TV and an Xbox Elite."

"It's a scholarship, for books and tuition and all that, not video games," Tate said.

"Hey, it's about the educational experience, Tate," Nathan said. "That's college."

"College is supposed to be a *learning* experience," Tate said.

"Do you know how *hard* it is to learn all ten maps in Gears of War 2?" Nathan asked. "You think this algebra stuff is tough? Sheesh. You ain't seen nothing."

The day couldn't pass quickly enough for Troy. When he got off the bus at the end of his driveway, he was surprised to see his mom's green VW bug waiting for him with its engine softly purring. He swung open the passenger door, and his mom told him to get in.

"I've got a surprise for you, Troy," she said, her face glowing.

No matter how hard he begged, she only grinned and shook her head as they spun down the dirt drive, kicking up grit and small stones. He could only imagine that it had to be his dad. His mom must have gotten the papers, then called him to work out the details for visitation; that's when she must have seen how closely his ideas meshed with hers. The two of them must now be united in their efforts to get Troy the best deal he could possibly get and to take advantage of the media frenzy.

His dream went up quickly, soaring like a lump of clay thrown into a towering vase the way his art teacher could do on a potter's wheel. He even dared to dream the ultimate dream that somehow, some way, his parents would end up back together.

When they turned the final bend in the road, the fragile tower of perfectly balanced clay wobbled violently, then crashed down into a mess of slimy mud.

CHAPTER THIRTY-ONE

IT WASN'T HIS FATHER'S orange Porsche but Seth's yellow H2 that was resting in the red clay patch in front of Troy's house. Beside it was a silver Cadillac sedan. On the porch, Seth stood talking to a man who wore a dark blue sweat suit, a baseball cap, and big glasses.

"Who is that?" Troy asked.

"Come on," his mom said, pulling to a stop and getting out of the car. "Let me introduce you."

Troy followed his mom up the front steps.

"Thank you so much for coming," his mom said to the man who blinked curiously at Troy. "Troy, this is John Marchiano. Mr. Marchiano came all the way from Las Vegas to help us."

Marchiano wore a big, friendly smile, and it seemed even brighter set in a face dark with razor stubble. His hair was long enough to spill free from the back of the baseball cap. He looked nothing like Troy's father, not even in the same league. Not big time at all.

"Troy, nice to meet you," Marchiano said, sticking out his hand so that Troy had to shake it. "Just call me John. You've got some mom, I'll tell you; and Seth has told me all about you. I'd love to help out."

Despite the sinking feeling in his stomach, Troy had to admit that there was something very open and friendly about the man; in any other setting, he would have liked him. Still, Troy said, "Thanks for coming, Mr. Marchiano, but I've got someone to help me already."

Marchiano blinked at Troy, then smiled uneasily and looked at Seth. Seth scowled and looked at Troy's mom. She glared at Troy.

"That is very rude, young man," she said. "You apologize."

"Tessa," Marchiano said, holding up both hands, "he doesn't have to apologize to me. He's the client. The client's never wrong."

Troy's mom curled her lips back off her teeth.

"I'm sorry," Troy said, looking down at his feet. "It's just that I've got someone I want to represent me already."

"What?" Seth said.

His mother gripped his upper arm and asked, "What are you talking about?"

Troy looked up at her, his eyes moist from the frustration and anger building inside him like a towering thunderstorm.

"My father," he said, choking out the words.

"Troy, stop that right now," his mother said, gripping his upper arm. "You don't even know the man."

"He's my father," Troy said. "What more do I have to know?"

Without another word, Troy tore open the front door and raced into the house. He dashed through the living room, around the corner, and into his own room, where he slammed the door shut. He slumped down on his bed, clenching two handfuls of hair. Through the door he could hear the voices of the adults as they entered the living room and talked among themselves. The sound of their voices rose and fell like the ocean surf. It went quiet for a minute. Troy heard a chickadee outside in the pines chattering away, then the rap of knuckles on his bedroom door.

"Go away," Troy said.

"Troy? It's me, John. I'm going, but I did want to just say a couple quick things to you, if you don't mind. Honestly, I came all the way from Las Vegas, and I'm heading right back there, and that's fine; but if I could tell you a couple things, maybe it'll help you down the line somewhere."

Troy got up, went to his door, and swung it open. John Marchiano stepped inside and looked around. His eyes came to rest on a picture of Troy and his gramps holding up a huge catfish between them, both of them straining, both smiling.

"Some fish," John said, stepping closer.

"That's my gramps," Troy said. "He knows all the good spots."

"I never had that," John said, "someone to take me fishing."

Troy nodded.

"Look," John said, taking a business card from his jacket pocket and handing it to Troy, "you ever need some advice, you give me a call. Your mom told me the whole thing about you and your dad, and I told her he should represent you."

"You did?" Troy said, searching the agent's eyes for a trick.

CHAPTER THIRTY-TWO

"SURE," JOHN SAID. "I lost my own dad when I was six, so I know what it's like at the end of a ball game and he's not there. So, if I could've gotten him back? You better believe he'd have been my agent, not that I needed one. I didn't play past college."

"You played?" Troy said.

"Syracuse University," John said with a grin. "Mostly a long snapper, but I wore the colors. Anyway, you keep that card. I'm not out running around looking for clients. Would I love to represent you? Sure. You got some special talent, and I'm betting this genius thing is only the beginning. From what Seth says, you'll be a player yourself if you stay healthy, but I don't recruit clients anymore. My law practice keeps me busy, and I get enough clients who come to me. I just came today because of Seth. He's a great guy, and he cares a lot about you. You need some advice sometime, you just call me."

John Marchiano turned to go.

"Mr. Marchiano," Troy said before John got out the door. "Do you think it's a good idea? I mean, my dad represents some big-time people, so he'll be good at this, right?"

"Call me John. Your dad will be great," John said, then his face became sober. "But you should never do business with family."

Troy rumpled his brow and tilted his head. "That doesn't make sense. Which is it?"

"Both," John said. "Your dad will do a great job with your deal. I have no doubt. You're right, G Money is in the big time, so your dad obviously knows his stuff. But, in the end, you'll regret it. Not because of the deal. I'm sorry. I can't lie to you. Agents make a lot of money, and a good one has to tell his client things the client doesn't like to hear. That's tough enough anyway, and family businesses are always a huge challenge. I've seen it before: a father representing his son. No, it never works out."

Troy frowned.

"But maybe you'll be different, Troy," John said cheerfully. "There's a first for everything, right?"

Troy studied John Marchiano's face, searching for the signs of the kind of trickster who would try to talk him out of working with his dad. But try as he might, all Troy saw was a friendly smile, and he knew instinctively that John Marchiano was speaking the truth as he knew it. Still, Troy wasn't about to let go of his dream of having a dad fully involved in his life.

"You have to dare to be different, right?" Troy said.

John gave him a short nod and said, "If you're the daring type, then you're right."

"I am," Troy said. "That's part of being a quarterback, too. You have to take chances sometimes to win the really big games."

"Yes, you do. Just don't throw an interception on the goal line. Good luck, Troy," John said, and he turned to go.

Troy followed the agent out into the living room. His mom and Seth looked up from where they sat on the couch.

"It's settled," Troy said. "Mr. Marchiano even says my dad's got what it takes to do this deal. If he represents G Money, he obviously knows his stuff."

John stopped in the middle of the floor and said, "I also told you that it's tough to do business with family."

Seth stood up and, with a pained expression, he said, "John, I'm really sorry I brought you out here."

John held up his hand. "Don't be. I'm glad I got the chance to meet Troy and talk to him. And he's got my card now in case he changes his mind."

Troy's mom stood, her back rigid, and said, "Troy's twelve, John, so this isn't necessarily the final word. He and I will be discussing this."

"Honestly, Tessa?" John said. "I meant it when I said Troy's the client. I know he's only twelve, but he acts a lot older, and this really is about him. I'm not trying to stick my nose in, but you might want to listen to him. If he wants his father to represent him, it's not like the man isn't qualified. I'm sorry; I know that's not what you or Seth wanted to hear from me, but I just finished telling Troy that a good agent sometimes has to say things his clients don't want to hear. Seth, I'll call you."

They all shook hands with John, thanking him before they followed him out. Troy got the door, pulling it open and gasping at the sight of a greasy-haired man with a pinched, angry face struggling up the final step. The man stood slouched over in a faded black suit coat, his age-spotted hands hanging at his sides.

The man wiped some sweat from his brow and narrowed his eyes, staring through the doorway at Troy's mom.

"Are you Tessa White?" he asked.

Troy's mom wrinkled her face and asked, "Who in the world are you?"

CHAPTER THIRTY-THREE

"YOU *ARE* TESSA WHITE?" the man asked again, nodding to himself and reaching into the back pocket of his pants, from where he removed what looked like a religious pamphlet.

"Yes," Troy's mom said, her eyes on the pamphlet that the man extended through the doorway.

The man shook the paper until she took it from him, then he gave her a curt nod, grunted, turned, and walked away. Troy watched the man climb into a faded blue compact car with a cracked windshield and a wire clothes hanger where the radio antenna should have been. The car sputtered to life and raced away, chomping up the gritty dirt track.

Troy turned his attention to the sound of his mother unfolding the paper.

"What is it?" Seth asked.

"Well, Troy," his mom said, rattling the paper with a sigh, "you got your wish; it's a lawsuit."

"What?" Troy asked.

"That was a process server," she said, nodding toward the dusty cloud in the driveway. "I'm being sued for custody, by your father."

Seth and John Marchiano both glanced at Troy, and he felt his face go warm.

"It's what you said he had to do," Troy said, angry that he felt ashamed.

She sighed and said, "Yes, I did."

"Well," John Marchiano said, "I'm off."

They all said good-bye. The agent offered a final, sad look, as if he knew something they didn't. Then he climbed into the rented Cadillac and followed the process server's trail of dust.

"So, I can see him?" Troy said as the dust settled, excitement creeping into his voice.

"I gave you my word," his mom said, sounding disappointed.

"Now?" Troy asked. "Can I call him? Can I see him?"

"Of course," his mom said quietly. She reached for Seth's hand, and they twined their fingers together. "But you tell him to knock it off now with the lawsuit."

The hopeless look she gave to Seth barely registered with Troy. He raced into the house and scooped up his mom's cell phone from the coffee table. Troy headed straight to his bedroom, where he could talk in private. Trembling, he took the card from its place beneath his mattress and dialed his father.

"Hello," Troy said, hesitant at the sound of his father's voice.

"Hey, Troy!" his father said, washing away all doubt with his enthusiasm. "She got it?"

"Yes, and I can see you."

"That's great," his father said. "You ready? I thought we'd get a big fat steak at Chops, but first I got a surprise that's going to knock you off your feet."

"Speaking of knocking," Troy said, "she wants you to knock it off with the lawsuit."

"Whatever it takes," he said.

"What surprise anyway?" Troy asked.

"If I told you, it wouldn't be a surprise, would it?" his father asked. "I'll be by to get you in about twenty minutes. You got a bathing suit, right?"

"Sure," Troy said, now truly mystified.

"Okay," his father said, "bring it."

CHAPTER THIRTY-FOUR

TROY CLUTCHED HIS ROLLED-UP bathing suit and pulled back the curtain to watch and wait. A heavy beam of late-day sun spilled through the glass, warming his cheek.

"You're not just running out there and taking off like a rocket, mister," his mom said. "He can come in and say hello and talk about some ground rules. This isn't a train station; it's our home."

Troy rolled his eyes. "Mom, please don't start with the ground rules."

"Don't *you* start, Troy," she said from her spot on the couch next to Seth. "You're twelve."

"How could I forget," Troy said, grumbling and turning his attention back to the window.

Over his shoulder, the clock on the wall wouldn't seem to move its hands. When the orange Porsche finally purred into the dirt patch, Troy swept aside the curtain. He pressed his face and hand against the warm glass. Troy's dad didn't even hesitate. He hopped out and vaulted up the steps in jeans, cowboy boots, and a silky button-down shirt. He pounded the door with three short, heavy knocks and stood there with his hair a wild tangle from the windy ride in the convertible.

"I'll get it," his mom said, pushing past Troy and swinging open the door.

"Drew," she said sarcastically, "what a surprise."

Troy's dad stepped inside, smoothed his hair, and wiped his feet.

"Good to see you, Tessa," he said, shaking her hand before he waved to Seth on the couch. "Seth."

He clasped Troy by the hand like a gladiator—instead of offering a formal shake—and pulled into a one-armed hug, clapping him on the back like a teammate.

"My man," his father said, and Troy beamed with pride.

"Drew," Troy's mom said, her hands going to her hips, "your 'man' has school tomorrow. I know you want to get to know each other a little, but he needs to be home by ten and—"

"Ten?" Troy said, raising his voice.

Drew held up a hand, silencing Troy. Then, in a somber voice, he said, "Of course, Tessa. I appreciate the opportunity here. You've obviously done a great job raising Troy. I'm happy to play by your rules."

Troy watched his mom's face relax. She nodded and said, "Thank you."

"And I don't want a free ride on this either," Drew said to her with serious eyes. "I expect that part of our arrangement will mean me helping support Troy—food, clothes, college when it's time, including the expenses you've already had."

Troy's mom opened her mouth to speak, but her eyes flickered at him and she closed it instead. Troy couldn't keep from grinning.

"Well," Drew said, rubbing his hands together as if warming them at a fire, "lots to do and not much time. Let me get him going and—"

"Going where, by the way?" Troy's mom asked.

"Chops for a steak," Drew said.

"But the bathing suit?" Troy's mom said.

"For a swim."

"Drew, I know it's warm out for November, but you're not jumping off any railroad bridges or anything crazy like that, right?" his mom asked.

"Me?" he said.

"Like the old days, remember?" she asked with one eyebrow raised.

She turned to Troy and said, "If there was water, your father would be in it, even if he had to jump off a bridge to get there. If we were at the beach in Biloxi, he'd swim out a mile and back just to prove he could. Once he jumped out of a raft down the Alabama River and met us at the dock."

"No rapids," he said, laughing lightly. "Strictly indoor swimming, but I want to surprise him about where. Okay?"

"Sure," Troy's mom said, and he thought she might have even smiled a bit. "And, Drew, I know you and Troy have spoken about having you represent him, but I want you to work through me on that."

"Mom," Troy said, "Mr. Marchiano said—"

"I'm your mom," she said, cutting him off. "If you want Drew to work on this deal, he'll be working on it through me or not at all."

Troy grumbled until his father said, "That makes perfect sense."

"It does?" Troy asked, looking up at him.

"Hey," Drew said, his smile flashing, "I'm your dad, but she's your mom, Troy. You gotta listen to her."

Troy's mom tilted her head, gazed at his father, and said, "Thank you, Drew."

"You sound surprised, Tessa," Drew said. "If I was so bad, Troy wouldn't even be here, would he?"

Troy's mom shrugged and said, "I guess not. You two have fun."

Troy and his dad waved good-bye to Seth. Troy kissed his mom, and they were off, with the top down.

Wind screamed past Troy's ears as his father sped down Route 400 against the grain of the commuters all leaving the city at the end of the workday.

"It's fast!" Troy shouted.

"You like it?" his father asked, glancing at him, downshifting, swerving into another lane, and surging ahead with even more power and speed.

"I liked the way you handled my mom," Troy shouted.

His father nodded and grinned and said, "Plenty of practice."

"How long did you guys go out?"

"Two years," his father said, his voice cutting through the wind.

"Pretty serious, huh?" Troy said.

"Serious enough to know how to work right around her," Drew said.

"What do you mean?" Troy shouted, a feeling of uncertainty creeping into the thrill of the wind and speed.

"She says I work through her," his dad said with a shrug. "That's fine. She can say what she likes, but you and I know that I'm running this deal. I already got Seth Cole lined up to interview you. You know who that is?"

"Seth Cole? The owner of the Jets?" Troy said. "Everyone knows him; he's superrich."

"The perfect team for you," Drew said. "Seth Cole knows how to win, and he doesn't care how much it costs."

"An interview?" Troy asked.

"To show him what you can do," Drew said, still shouting. "When he sees what you can do, we might have a deal before we leave New York."

"New York?" Troy said, his heart skipping all over the place.

His dad nodded and said, "The big time, for real. New York is the center of the world."

"How do we get there?" Troy asked.

"Seth Cole's got a Global 5000. A big private jet. It'll be here for us in the morning."

"But school," Troy said.

His dad waved a hand as if dismissing the question.

Troy digested that in silence until his dad exited the highway and pulled to a stop on the street beside the Georgia Aquarium. The sun had disappeared behind the buildings, and the early evening air had begun to cool.

"This is it," his dad said, slipping out of the car. "Bring your suit."

"What?" Troy said, fumbling with the handle. "You can't swim in an aquarium."

"Most people can't," his father said. "But we aren't most people, are we?"

CHAPTER THIRTY-FIVE

"**I TOLD YOU G** Money has the keys to this city," Troy's father said.

"But," Troy said, hustling to keep up along the concrete sidewalk, "it's a fish tank. You can't just swim in it, no matter who you are."

"Well," his father said, still walking, "technically speaking, we're not going to swim; we're going to *dive*. But you could say swim."

"Dive?" Troy said. They had reached the door to the entrance now, and his dad stepped up to the members window, where he gave his name to the person inside. A woman wearing a blue blazer and carrying a radio appeared, introducing herself as Christine Swimmer, the assistant manager of the aquarium.

"Right this way," she said.

"I don't know," Troy said, whispering to his dad. "I had a goldfish once, and they make a disgusting mess."

His father smiled down at him and tousled his hair.

"Don't worry," he said, "you're going to love this. I promise. It's a once-in-a-lifetime thing. You'll be in a wet suit and breathing through a tube."

They climbed a set of back stairs and emerged into a huge open space with a salty marsh smell like the time he'd gone crab fishing off the bridge leading to Jekyll Island on the coast. A metal mesh floor surrounded a round tank of water bigger than any pool Troy had ever seen. He sniffed and watched as a young woman wearing a wet suit dug her hands into a huge cooler, coming up with fistfuls of dead and bloody fish, which she tossed into the water. Colors flashed beneath the water's churning surface, and two dark shadows cruised through the frenzy like a bad dream.

"Sharks," his father said, nodding at the water. "You ever hear of that saying?"

"What saying?" Troy asked.

"'Swim with the sharks'?" his father said, pointing to the water, then at two sets of wet suits, masks, and fins hanging from hooks on the wall. "Don't worry. It's perfectly safe. They just ate. Come on."

Troy followed his father through a door and into a locker room, where they changed into their bathing suits, then returned to the tank.

"Charlie and Melissa will help you out," Christine Swimmer said, and two young people in wet suits appeared and showed them how to get into their gear.

Troy found himself stepping into a wet suit, wiggling his feet and hands to push them through their openings, and then sucking in his breath as Charlie zipped up the suit from behind. Troy slipped his feet into flippers and helped fix the mask on his face. Then Charlie strapped a belt around Troy's middle that had pouches filled with plastic-covered weights. When Troy's father put an arm around his shoulders, it almost made Troy's worry disappear, but not quite.

"Okay," his father said, "here's the thing: You're scared."

"I'm not scared," Troy said.

"Yeah, you are," his father said happily, "but that's okay. That's the point of this. It scares me, too. Look at that whale shark."

Troy looked to where his dad was pointing. A shadow twice as long as Gramps's fishing boat cruised across the tank. Troy gulped.

"No way should we be jumping into the water with that thing," his father said. "It's a primal fear. It comes from our forefathers, all the way back to the cavemen. People who mixed with things like that got eaten. Only the ones smart enough to be afraid survived."

He looked at Troy, and Troy couldn't help feeling confused.

"The big-time people overcome that fear," his father said. "They don't pretend it doesn't exist. They deal with it and dominate it. They take the stage. They write the great novel. They drop back and throw the touchdown pass that wins the game. It's all scary, because most people don't make it. Most people fail, so they never even try.

"This is just a symbol of what we've got ahead of us, you and me. There's going to be scary things—things big and dark that you can't quite see—that you'll have to jump in the tank with. It starts here. Come on. I'll be with you. Trust me. I told you I've always wanted a son. I'm sure not going to lose you this quick."

Drew reached for a long yellow hose coiled neatly on the side of an air compressor. He flipped the switch so that it whirred to life. "Here, you put this regulator in your mouth. Stick with me. Charlie will be in there with us, too. I promise, this is something you'll never forget; and when you come out of there, you'll never be the same."

Charlie gave Troy some basic instructions and showed him how to go in with his hand covering his mask as well as the regulator, which stuck out of his mouth like a small can of tuna. Troy watched as his father shrugged into a buoyancy vest with its own air tank and weight pockets, then nodded at Troy and stepped into the water. Troy bit down on the rubber mouthpiece, covered his face, and stepped off the ledge, plunging into a swirl of bubbles and the kingdom of monsters.

Troy felt his father's strong grip on his upper arm, and he turned to see Drew's questioning look and the "okay" sign he made with his fingers. Troy nodded and signaled "okay" back, even though he felt his heart bumping in his throat.

Beneath them, the spotted whale shark swept its tail back and forth like a pendulum. All around, the smaller and more colorful fish zoomed back and forth. Troy and his dad sank slowly, the coral formations crowding in on them. The hiss and click of a million air bubbles exploded all around them.

Then Troy's dad nudged him and pointed, and there it came: a ten-foot hammerhead shark, with its nasty sneer and its dull dead eyes, snaking up toward them through the water. The pale chin dropped open, and Troy could see the jagged rows of teeth. Without thinking, he broke for the surface, kicking madly, but his father held him down. He wrapped his muscular legs around Troy's legs, pinning him in a human vise so that Troy stopped struggling.

The shark came right at them, its mouth grinning wildly at the sight of Troy's terror. Its eyes seemed to dance at the thought of his blood.

CHAPTER THIRTY-SIX

THE MASSIVE FISH VEERED off and swam away.

Troy felt his body go limp. His father's regulator exploded with bubbles and a burst of underwater laughter. Then his father jiggled an "okay" sign in front of Troy's face, nodding his head to ask if Troy was all right. Troy held up his own sign, weak but with the warmth of avoided danger blossoming in his chest.

The reef sharks, sawfish, barracudas, and even the docile whale shark soon became novelties, like puppet dragons hung backstage after a show. Even the nasty hammerhead soon proved he wanted less to do with the divers than they wanted with him. And once when Charlie wasn't looking, Troy even flicked a hand at it, causing it to flinch and hurry away, wagging its tail like a puppy.

That's when Troy noticed the evening crowd. Ordinary people—men, women, kids, and teenagers—all pressed to the glass, all pointing at them, the ones who swam with the sharks.

When Charlie signaled for them to head up, Troy felt a disappointment he couldn't have imagined a half hour before. Still, when they broke the surface, the exhilaration of it all made him whoop and slap a high five with his father before they even got out of the tank. They shed their gear and changed back into their clothes in the locker room, his father toweling off with brisk strokes. Before they left, Troy noticed his father slip folded bills of money to the people who had helped them, even Christine Swimmer. When they broke out into the evening light on the sidewalk, he asked about it.

"Did you have to pay them off?" Troy asked.

His father chuckled and said, "No. The aquarium did that as a favor to me. I helped set up G Money to do a charity event for them. Those people got the word from way up high to give us the VIP treatment. They do dives like that for other people, but it takes a long time to get in. I just gave them that money as a tip, just to say thanks."

"That's how they do it in the big time?" Troy asked.

"Exactly how," his father said. "When you make big, big money, you don't mind throwing it around a little. People appreciate it, and it comes back to you in ways you can't imagine."

"Do you have big money?"

His father gave him a knowing grin and waved to the orange Porsche on the street. "Big enough so I don't talk about it," he said.

"Sorry," Troy said.

"No, that's okay. You're my son."

They ate thick steaks at Chops and had lobster tails drenched in butter. Troy dug into a strawberry short-cake, while his father had a glass of thick purple wine called port. On the drive home, Troy begged to have the top down, even though the temperature had dropped sharply without the sun. As they got off the highway near Troy's home, he pointed at the clock on the dash-board.

"It's only nine," he said.

"I know," his father said. "I'll get you home early."

Troy's face fell, and his father reached over to muss his hair.

"Don't look like that," his father said. "It's not because I don't want to be with you. It's the exact opposite. I get you home early and it does two things. First, it puts your mom in a good mood; and second, it gives me time to explain to her why she needs to let you miss school tomorrow."

"To fly out to New York?" Troy asked, excited now. "You really think she'll let me?"

"I know her pretty well, Troy," Drew said, his eyes

narrowing at the road ahead, "and, like I said, I haven't forgotten how to deal with her. Yeah, I think we got a pretty good chance she'll let you go, but we'll see. It's just like football. You never know for sure you've won until that final gun."

CHAPTER THIRTY-SEVEN

THEY PULLED UP INTO the dirt patch in front of Troy's house, and Drew snuggled the Porsche right up next to the VW bug.

"Excellent," Drew said, his eyes scanning all around them. "Seth's got some manners."

"What do you mean?" Troy asked.

"A lot of guys in his shoes would be upset about all this," Drew said, sitting and looking at the small salt-box house. "The old boyfriend showing up. Father of the kid. Me and your mom? We've got some catching up to do, and we sure couldn't do it with Seth hanging around. I respect him."

"You mean, like, he'd be jealous?" Troy asked, his heart thumping. "Like you and my mom getting back together?"

"I doubt that," Drew said, chuckling softly until he looked at Troy's face, "but you never know, right?"

"That's what I was thinking," Troy said, following his father as he hopped out of the car, then trailing him up onto the porch.

"Okay," Drew said, taking hold of Troy's shoulder. "You let me do the talking in there. Just do what you normally do."

"Like get ready for bed and say good night?" Troy asked. "But how do I know if I'm going to New York with you?"

"You don't," Drew said, "but you trust me. If there's any way of you going, it won't happen unless you just go to bed like you're not expecting anything other than a day of algebra, or whatever it is you take in whatever grade you're in."

"Seventh," Troy said.

His dad shrugged and angled his head at the glow from the big front window.

Troy opened the door and wasn't surprised to see his mom reading a book on the couch with her feet curled up underneath her. Drew stepped inside but stayed on the mat.

"Okay if I come in?" Drew said in a voice Troy hadn't heard before.

"Sure," his mom said, closing the book but without getting up.

"Well," Troy said, extending a hand to his father, "thanks . . ."

Troy blushed, unsure of what to call him.

"Thanks, Dad?" Drew said, raising his eyebrows and then grinning as he shook Troy's hand. "You may as well get used to it."

"Thanks . . . Dad," Troy said, and it felt oh so good.

Even his mom smiled, and Troy kissed her and said good night. On his way into the hallway toward the bathroom, he heard his dad ask, "Mind if I sit?"

"No," his mom said. "Please."

From the corner of his eye, Troy saw his father sit on the couch, careful to leave an empty cushion between them before he turned and winked at Troy. Troy hurried out of sight.

When he was ready for bed, Troy moved slowly down the hall, his ears aching to decipher the low murmur of his parents' voices. He stopped and listened hard, until they went silent and his mom shot her voice his way.

"Troy? Get to bed."

Troy scuttled into his room, closing the door and plastering his ear to its smooth, cool surface.

Nothing.

For quite some time he paced his room, listening for something, anything. He considered slipping out through the window but knew better. He made up wizardly devices he wished he had, things that could snake silently through the air vents with a microphone or detect words from the vibrations of sound moving through walls. In the end he lay down on his bed, yawned, and waited for the sound of his mother's bath and the water groaning through the pipes. When she went to bed, he could sneak out to the kitchen phone and call his father to get the scoop. His mind whirled around the different possibilities between his parents, his contract, the TV interviews he would soon be doing, and his entire future.

The thirst to know what they were saying and doing battled with his drooping eyelids and the yawns that snuck up out of his throat. Eventually, he surrendered to exhaustion with the final thought that if he allowed himself to close his eyes, the next time they opened he would know his fate.

CHAPTER THIRTY-EIGHT

TROY AND HIS FATHER sped down not the interstate that led to the Atlanta airport but a back road that took them to the DeKalb Peachtree Airport, a place his dad said was less than a half hour from Troy's home.

"How'd you do it?" Troy asked.

His father shifted the sunglasses on his face, then smoothed the slicked-back hair that held its shape even with the top down.

"Magic," his father said.

"Come on," Troy said, stuffing a knuckle into his yawn. "My mom let me miss Home Ec yesterday and that went into the *Guinness Book of World Records*. She doesn't let me miss a day of school for anything."

"Anything except Seth Cole, who happens to own the New York Jets," his father said as he spun the wheel.

They turned in through an open chain-link gate and came to rest outside a white concrete terminal with an air traffic control tower sprouting from one corner like the turret of a castle.

"It had to be more than that," Troy said.

"I can't teach you all my tricks," his father said, grinning.

Two glass doors yawned open as they stepped inside the terminal, following a red carpet to the desk where a young woman asked for their names. She showed them to a doorway where a man in a blue jumpsuit waited with a golf cart. They climbed into the backseat and the cart lurched forward, dodging through a jungle of jet airplanes whose tight white skins gleamed in the sunlight. Troy had to blink to study their different designs and the barrel-shaped engines each one of them sported in pairs.

Once through the jungle, they emerged on the edge of the runway near a bigger plane, with an engine the size of his mom's VW bug. Its stairs were down. The pilot next to them stood checking a clipboard. He tipped his hat to Troy and his dad before following them up the stairs and into the airplane.

A man in a different kind of uniform greeted them politely and told them to let him know if there was anything they needed. Troy lost his breath when he smelled the leather and saw the gleaming brass and the swirling grain of the dark wood. The cabin looked like an elegant living room, and Troy didn't know what to do, even when his father flopped down into a plush leather seat and extended his feet.

"Where should I go?" he asked, directing his voice away from the attendant and trying not to sound like a fool.

"Anywhere you want," his father said, removing a laptop from his briefcase and booting it up.

"What about everyone else?" Troy asked, looking about at the empty room.

His father glanced around, then smiled. "Oh. There isn't anyone else, buddy. It's just us."

The sound of the door being pulled shut from the front proved his father was right. Troy sat down in the other big chair, facing forward like his dad. While his father's fingers jittered across the computer's keyboard, Troy studied the big screen on the wall in front of them. Various maps and charts took turns filling the screen like a slide show. The attendant hurried to finish fussing in the small kitchen area by the front and ducked out to say that he'd be with them in just a blink.

The plane turned fast, and the engines howled, thrusting them forward. Troy felt the wheels leave the earth. Up they shot, nearly straight, engines groaning under the strain so that Troy's stomach clenched with the fear of dropping from the sky like a brick.

Instead, they sailed ever higher until they began to level out. As they approached the Georgia mountains, the earth below lay spread out like a rumpled blanket. His father didn't even look up.

"You can get internet service?" Troy asked.

"Yup."

"You working?" Troy asked.

His father glanced up and said, "For you, I am."

"Doing what?" Troy asked.

"Whipping them up."

"Whipping who?"

"Them," his father said, waving his hand at the world below. "The teams, the media, the fans."

Troy tilted his head, and his father's hands rose up from the keyboard to gesture as he spoke.

"Remember that hockey player who broke his neck, and they thought he'd never walk again but he did?" his father asked.

"The one from the Blackhawks?"

"Right, him," his father said. "I sold the movie rights to that story. Got him half a million dollars."

"I think I saw that movie on TV," Troy said.

His father's eyes gleamed. "The day after he took his first step, I had ten TV cameras at the hospital and twenty print reporters. After that I started whipping up the producers and the studios. I got five times what that story would have been worth if I'd just put it out there. You can't just put things out there; you have to whip them up. You make up a number and say you already got an offer from some big name. Then the rest get scared they're going to miss something. They get hungry. They stop thinking with their heads, and they let their stomachs take over. They drive the price up into the stars. That's when I ink the deal."

"Is that," Troy said, hesitating, "honest?"

His father shrugged, grinned, and said, "I don't know. That's being an agent."

He offered Troy a final nod before turning his attention back to the computer screen. Troy studied his dad's flurry of typing and then turned to look down at the wrinkled mountains below.

Troy watched the mountains, countryside, and small towns and cities slide by beneath them. Still, it was sooner than he imagined it would be when the buildings of New York City appeared in the distance, surrounded by water, closely packed together and stretching for the sky. Troy stared at the enormous city on their approach—marveling at its buildings, its bridges, and the pale green Statue of Liberty poking up from its harbor. His eyes couldn't get big enough to take it all in, and he craned his neck for one last glimpse of the skyline as they took the final plunge, then thumped down to land at the airport. The plane taxied to a stop just outside the terminal. They descended the steps and his father searched the area outside the chain-link fence, smiling with a satisfied nod at the sight of the cameras and the milling crowd of reporters who surrounded a long black limousine just outside the terminal.

"Is that for us?" Troy asked.

His father grinned and gestured for him to walk on. "Son, welcome to the Big Apple."

CHAPTER THIRTY-NINE

FROM INSIDE THE TERMINAL, Troy eyed the flailing mob through two big glass doors.

"What do we do?" Troy asked.

His father looked up from the BlackBerry he'd been working with since they walked inside. Holding it forth, he said, "Here's what we do. We say nothing. I'll push through that mob like a lead blocker. You tuck in behind me, and I'll get you into the limo. I just got a text here that says we might be doing the David Letterman show. How's that sound?"

"What?" Troy said, choking with nerves and uncertain if it was because of the crowd outside or the thought of appearing on *Letterman.*

"Yeah," his father said, pumping a fist, "I got them. This is so big, the entire country will be watching.

161

Everyone will be talking. It's more than sports. It's the lifeblood of America. You'll be a superstar."

"The big time?" Troy asked.

"Oh yeah," his father said.

Troy hesitated, glancing at the crowd, and said, "But you got all these reporters to come here, right? How can we just push past them without talking?"

"Believe me," his father said, "they'll get over it. They're used to it. They know the game. They'll all have a shot of you pushing through the crowd and saying nothing. It'll yank their chains. But trust me, it'll make tonight even bigger."

"Should I at least say that I'm sorry?" Troy said, worrying.

His father swatted the air and said, "Naw. Come on. Follow me. Don't worry. These maggots will get over it."

The word "maggots" startled Troy, but his father gave him a wink and a nod, and he couldn't do anything other than follow him as instructed, actually gripping a handful of his father's shirt as they burst out of the terminal and pushed through the mob and into the waiting limousine.

Once Troy was inside, his father turned to the angry crowd and held up both hands to speak.

"Hey," his father said, "I'm sorry about the rush, but you folks know Seth Cole and his reputation. We're late to meet him, and this is shaping up to be an eight-figure deal. The team that signs Troy White is guaranteed to be the next NFL dynasty, and you can quote me on that."

Troy's father seemed to enjoy slamming the door shut on the questions that rained down on him. He smacked the lock down and barked at the driver to get going. Troy turned around to watch as a handful of cameramen scrambled after the limo, filming their departure from the airport. As they approached the Lincoln Tunnel, Troy gasped at the sight of New York City up close. From the plane he had no idea how big things really were.

Then the limo twisted around and dipped into the tunnel, which seemed to run forever beneath the Hudson River. When they emerged into the canyon of buildings, Troy was amazed. He twisted his neck so he could look up, catching sight of only random patches of sky.

"It's so big," Troy said as they drove on and on, into the heart of the city, up Sixth Avenue and toward the spindly, bare branches of the trees in Central Park. Through the park they went, and Troy couldn't keep his jaw from dropping at the mystery of so many trees in the middle of a city that seemed to never end. He had so many questions, but his father was intent on the BlackBerry, where his thumbs flickered like the mouth parts of a feeding crayfish.

When they came out of the park, the car took a right

onto Fifth Avenue and cruised down several blocks until they came to a mansion with cast-iron gates and a decorative fence. Its magnificence reminded Troy of something he'd see in a Social Studies book about European kings and queens.

"This is a house?" Troy asked.

His father looked up from his BlackBerry, squinted his eyes at the fountain spraying water from the center of the circular drive, and said, "It's Seth Cole's house. I don't know if it's a home. 'The owner without a soul,' they call him."

"Sounds scary," Troy said.

"He blows his nose on hundred-dollar bills," his father said. "Money means nothing to him."

"So, he'll outbid everyone?" Troy asked.

"That's the plan."

For the first time, Troy realized that if all this really happened, he and his mom would no longer be living in the small saltbox tucked into the pinewoods on the outskirts of Atlanta. They might be living in a big house like Seth Halloway's, and it might not be in Atlanta at all. Tate and Nathan wouldn't be going with him, nor would Seth Halloway.

Troy swallowed hard. He thought about suggesting that if Mr. Langan could come close to what the Jets owner offered, maybe he should stay where he was, but the words didn't come out. A man in a suit and ascot tie marched down the front steps of the mansion to open the limousine's door. Inside they went, through a grand entrance and up a staircase as wide as Troy's driveway back home. Their feet fell silent on thick rugs, the kind Troy knew people called Oriental. The silent man in the suit showed them into a large room with walls and ceiling that looked like a checkerboard of gleaming golden wood. The shine of the wood, like the luster of every lamp, leather cushion, and book binding, reminded Troy of the Falcons' executive offices and the times he'd met with Mr. Langan. Everything was spotless, rich, and elegant. At one end of the rectangular room was a broad desk facing out. They sat on a long leather coach perpendicular to the desk in the middle of the room and facing the tall windows. The man in the suit fidgeted with some switches on the wall, and panels slid down over the windows, blocking out the light, while a screen the size of Troy's front porch hummed down from out of the ceiling.

Troy looked around as the lights dimmed. The image of a football game—frozen in time but as clear and sharp as if he and his father were sitting in the Jets' stadium—appeared on the screen, and there they sat, whispering.

"He wants me to predict the plays?" Troy asked.

"I told you," his father said. "You need to show him what you can do is all. Why? Nervous?"

"A little," Troy said, looking around the room and noticing for the first time a stuffed polar bear standing ten feet tall in the corner of the room behind them. Its fangs and claws were bared and ready to strike.

"Well, this can't be as much pressure as when you were at the dome on Sunday with the Falcons down by two touchdowns," his father said.

"I guess," Troy said.

"Remember the sharks?" his father asked in a low voice. "Don't worry, I'm right here with you."

Troy didn't get the chance to respond because a door behind the desk opened and a slim man wearing an olive green suit entered the room. His probing eyes locked onto Troy's. Without blinking or looking away, the owner crossed the carpet and offered his hand. Troy, like his father, stood up to greet the Jets' famous but mysterious owner.

"Seth Cole," Troy's father said in a friendly way, "it's a pleasure to meet you."

Troy felt a surge of pride as his father stood toe-to-toe with Seth Cole, matching his intense stare and firm handshake.

"The pleasure will be mine," Seth Cole said with a doubtful smile, "if this young man can do everything the papers say he can do. I don't believe the papers, though. My past life taught me that. They're billboards, and you can buy them like ad space."

"And still, they sometimes prove to be incredibly

accurate," Troy's dad said to Seth Cole before he snuck a wink at Troy.

Seth Cole scooped up a remote from the lamp table next to the leather couch and said, "Let's see."

CHAPTER FORTY

SETH COLE SAT DOWN so that Troy was seated between the owner and Drew. The owner pointed the remote and the Jets' defense—suspended in the middle of a New England Patriots pass play—went into action. Seth Cole let four plays run without stopping before he said, "Well?"

Troy cleared his throat and said, "It's like the weatherman. I see patterns, and then I know what the plays will be."

"But it takes time for the patterns to emerge," the Jets' owner said, nodding. "Yes, I know. I told you; I've read the papers. So, I don't see why a team—with the right technology—couldn't break the patterns and render you next to worthless."

Troy's stomach knotted up, and Troy looked at his

father. Drew put a strong hand on Troy's shoulder and held it tight.

"Having played a little football myself," his father said, "I can tell you that if you break certain patterns, then you'll lose for sure. If it's third down and you've got ten yards to go, for instance, you better pass or the odds of getting a first down are about one in thirty."

"Well put," the owner said, and he ran another play.

"Strong side draw," Troy said, the knowledge coming to him before Seth Cole could advance to the next play.

The Patriots ran a strong side draw.

"Deep post to Randy Moss," Troy said, and they ran it.

"Weak side inside trap," Troy said.

When the Patriots ran the play Troy called, Seth Cole flicked off the video. They sat in total darkness for a minute, and Troy shifted in his seat.

The owner cleared his throat and said, "People are uncomfortable with situations they're not used to. That's human nature. Sitting in the dark, for instance. Something that for me is as natural as sitting under the noon sun. Are you uncomfortable, Troy?"

Troy hesitated, glancing at the blackness where his father sat before he said, "A little. I guess."

"Yes," the owner said, "I'd think a lot. And I'm going to ask you to do something you haven't done before, too. Because if I'm going to invest the kind of money I think you're asking for, I don't want to pay it to someone who can't adjust. In life, things never stay the same. In football, you have to adjust quickly, even when you're under pressure."

"Okay," Troy said after another moment of silence.

"Good," the owner said.

Troy heard a click, and the screen glowed to life, showing a frozen picture of the Jets. It didn't take Troy more than a half second to recognize that the difference was that now the screen showed the Jets' offense.

"We have what a lot of people are calling the best young offensive weapon in the game," the owner said.

"Thane Lewis?" Troy asked.

"Yes," the owner said, "and if I'm going to pay you a fortune to work for my team, I want to take advantage of that talent. I've been thinking about your ability, and I'd like to see if it works for both sides of the ball. I know defenses react to what they see on the offense; but without motion, I'm wondering if you can predict what coverage a defense is in, and if you could signal something like that in to a player like Thane Lewis. If he knew the coverage, I don't think there's a defense in the league that could stop him. Could you read a defense like that?"

Troy had to stick his hands under his legs to keep from jumping out of his seat and shouting. A thrill shot through him, and he nodded his head.

"I know I can," he said.

"You know?" The owner's voice was laced with amusement.

"I play football, Mr. Cole," Troy said.

"I heard that."

"I play quarterback," Troy added. "We just won the state championship on Saturday. A lot of it is because I know exactly what the coverage is going to be when I step up to the line. I can throw it, too."

"So, why haven't the Falcons used you to help their offense?" Seth Cole asked. "Or have they?"

"No," Troy said. "I guess nobody really thought about it. Seth—not you, Mr. Cole, but Seth Halloway—he's the one who got the team to even give me a chance, and he's their middle linebacker. So I just have been helping the defense."

"Then let's see if you can help the Jets' offense," the owner said.

Troy turned his attention to the screen. Three plays later, he began to call the defensive coverage. The owner let him go for five plays before he pressed another button that brought up the lights. His eyes bore into Troy's, and a pleasant smile curled at the corners of his mouth.

"I like it. I like it very much," he said, then turned to Troy's dad. "How much?"

Troy's father scratched his chin and, without dropping the owner's gaze, said, "The Falcons are talking eight figures over three years."

"Ten million over three years?" Seth Cole said, his eyebrows disappearing beneath the eaves of dark hair.

"At a minimum," Troy's father said. "Eight figures is the range."

"Will they give you fifteen?" Seth Cole asked.

"Maybe," Troy's father said.

"No. They won't," Seth Cole said, grinning and shaking his head.

"I can't say," Troy's father said.

"I will."

"You will what?" his father asked.

"Give you fifteen million," Seth Cole said, glancing at Troy, "for three years. But I have to have an option for three more years at twenty, with a right of first refusal after that."

Troy's head spun. The room seemed to float around him. It was all so big, so fast. For some reason he couldn't stop thinking about G Money's pool.

"How much up front?" Troy heard his father ask.

"How much do you want?" Seth Cole said.

"Ten," Troy's father said.

Seth Cole burst into a short fit of laughter before he took a breath and said, "Five million up front, but you don't leave this room without agreeing to the deal. Do you have the authority?"

"Yes, his mother agreed to follow my lead on this," Troy's dad said. "I'll need her signature, though. She's his legal guardian, but she's trusting me to cut the deal."

"Very good," the owner said.

"But I can't just agree to something without considering all the options," Troy's father said.

The owner stared for a moment, his eyes sweeping across Troy's father's face as if he were reading a book.

"His mother agreed to follow your lead. You can do anything you want," Seth Cole said, his voice soft but deadly serious. "You're the agent. You're the lawyer. You're the *father*."

"How did you know that?" Troy asked, unable to stop himself.

Seth Cole looked at Troy with empty eyes. "I'm an investor. I make it my business."

They sat in silence for a few moments before Troy's father said, "Well, I really can't—"

Seth Cole stood abruptly and shook Troy's hand. "Very nice to meet you, Troy. I wish you the best of luck. Drew, maybe next time."

Seth Cole shook Troy's father's hand and slipped away, striding for the door behind the desk. Troy looked at his father and saw the anguish on his face.

"Wait!" Troy's father said.

But Seth Cole kept going.

CHAPTER FORTY-ONE

"SETH," TROY'S FATHER SAID. "Wait! You can't."

Seth Cole wrapped his fingers around the shiny gold doorknob and gripped it before he stopped, let it go, and turned around. The owner said nothing; he simply went to the desk and removed some papers from the drawer, then plucked a pen from its holder and strode back across the room, extending them both to Troy's dad before placing them down on the granite top of the low table in front of the couch.

"The mother will have to sign the actual contract if she's Troy's legal guardian," Seth said, "but what I want from you—his agent—is this letter of intent. Troy should sign it, too. Because I want your word, both of you, that this is going to happen. That will do. I built my fortune on trusting people."

"He can't start until next season," Troy's father said. "You know that, right?"

"No," Troy said, "I can't."

"I understand that," Seth Cole said. "I'll be rooting for the Falcons in the Super Bowl."

Troy's dad examined the letter, then picked up the pen. He chuckled and shook his head and gave Troy a wink, then signed the paper. Troy, who had been holding his breath since he didn't know when, let it out. His father pushed the papers his way and handed him the pen.

"Go ahead," his father said. "You can sign it, too. Let's do this right."

Troy held the pen and placed his free hand flat on top of the paper, studying his father's wavy signature.

"What about my mom?" Troy said.

"If your dad says she's on board," Seth Cole said, "I seriously doubt she's going to argue with this deal."

"She's in the PR department for the Falcons," Troy said.

"She won't need to work another day in her life," Troy's dad said.

"She likes to work," Troy said. "I want her to have a job with the team."

"No," Seth Cole said, his face set in stone. "I don't do that. I can have the team give her an interview, but that's all I'll promise. I can get her interviews with every one of the TV networks and half the ad agencies on Madison Avenue, but I don't hire people to do favors. No one wins. Ever. I'm sorry."

Troy looked up at Seth Cole, whose face remained unreadable. Seth Cole stared at Troy hard, and it was as if he could read Troy's thoughts: the fear of leaving his friends and the world he knew fighting with the wild dream of being rich, his parents a couple, and all of them living in the big time.

Troy nodded, then put pen to paper and signed his name.

CHAPTER FORTY-TWO

"I KNOW *LETTERMAN* ISN'T locked in, but you don't really want me to just drop it, do you?" Troy's father asked, his face full of disbelief.

Troy felt his eyes grow moist and he looked away, ashamed for not knowing why but knowing in his heart that the only thing he wanted was to be alone with his mom. At the same time, he didn't want to disappoint his father.

"I just want to go home," Troy said, trying to sound strong. "I've got practice tonight. I almost forgot."

"Because I can make this thing happen, Troy. And buddy," his father said, laughing, "you don't need practice. You don't need anything except to figure out how you're going to spend your money."

"It's not just about the money," Troy said.

"What are you," his father said, "in shock or something?"

"I just don't want to go on TV," Troy said, amazed at how quickly the notion of having the entire country see him, Troy White, on TV had turned sour. "We don't need to whip them up anymore now that we've got the deal. I just want to go home. That's all. I've got football. Can't we?"

Troy's father looked sadly down at his BlackBerry. He punched in some words, waited, then nodded his head and slowly said, "I had a lot of media lined up, but you're right; the real purpose was to hype the deal. Yeah, we can go back. It's okay. Whatever you want, Troy."

Troy wanted to tell his father that it certainly didn't feel like whatever he wanted. It felt as if he'd been swept up in a tornado and didn't have any more say than a tattered sheet of newspaper spinning in the dust and leaves.

"Home," Troy said, and that's where they went.

The plane ride back wasn't as magical as the ride to New York. Troy stared out the window. The afternoon sun glinted off ponds, lakes, and rivers below, leaving the impression not of golden treasure but of worthless glitter scattered carelessly in the wake of a cheap parade.

The attendant offered sandwiches to them both, but Troy's dad waved him off and Troy didn't feel hungry at all. His father worked the laptop twice as hard as he had on the morning flight, something Troy hadn't thought possible. But even as they touched down at DeKalb Peachtree Airport, his father pounded away on the keys without looking up. Finally, though, when the big plane came to a halt, his father did look up to blink and smile and give Troy one of his winks.

"Are you writing apology emails to all the reporters?" Troy asked.

"Apologies?" his father said. "Heck, no. I'm moving money. Making deals. Communicating with my partners. Making the money is just the beginning. Now you've got to put it to work."

"Work?" Troy said.

"Sure," his father said. "Investments. Tax shelters. Trusts. Real estate. Hedge funds. Money is like soap. You let it sit there and the rain washes it away. Time whittles money down to nothing. You have to protect it. Inflation. Taxes. All that."

"You do that, too?" Troy asked.

"Naw," his father said, tapping a finger against his temple. "I'm no expert, but I know people who are. The best. Big time. All of them. I've already got one of my partners setting up an offshore corporation for us—or you, I mean."

"Corporation?" Troy asked as they stood to go.

"Big time," his father said.

Troy followed him out the door, thanking the flight attendant who'd been so nice and stepping into the bright Atlanta sunshine.

When they arrived at Troy's house, his mom's car was sitting by itself in the red clay patch. Troy's dad hopped out and eagerly made for the front door, where he knocked but then went right in.

"Tessa!" he shouted. "We did it! You're rich!"

Troy's mom appeared from the kitchen, wiping her hands on an apron, her face dusted with smudges of baking flour.

"I've been rich," she said.

"Not like this you haven't," his father said, glancing around the tiny room before putting his arms around her and hugging her and spinning her around until she finally managed to push him away, laughing.

"Okay," she said, her laughter trailing off, "what's the offer?"

"Something too good to refuse," his father said. "So we agreed in principle. I said that of course we had to get you to sign off, but we gave our word."

"Your word that what?" she asked.

"That we'd do this deal," Troy's father said. "I know I said I wouldn't, but I had to."

"You were just to get things going," she said, her voice sounding empty with disbelief. "To 'whip them up,' you said, 'get the bidding started.' We have to check with the Falcons. After everything they've done for us?"

"They'll never match it," his father said. "Mr. Langan is rich, but he won't throw money around like this,

Tessa. Just listen. You never listen. It's more than we dreamed. It's more than I asked for. It's a fortune! Fifteen million dollars, maybe thirty-five, forty, even fifty before it's over. Who knows?"

"What are you talking about?" she asked.

"Troy, tell her," his father said. "Tell her why we had to give him our word and kind of lock this thing down."

Troy looked from one of his parents to the other and nodded. "Seth Cole told us either sign it or he wasn't interested."

"I threw out the idea of eight figures, shooting for the moon," his father said. "No one actually offered me that. I was posturing, and he, well, he just made an incredible offer. So, we did it. Don't tell me you don't see how huge this is? It's everything Troy's dreamed of, everything he deserves. And we gave our word. You can't ask us to back out on that. That's not the example you want to set for Troy. How could you be looking at me like that?"

Troy's mom wasn't smiling. She wadded her apron up tight and shook her head. Speaking softly but with a full portion of disgust, she said, "You think it's all about money? It's not. There are other things."

"What other things are there when we're talking fifteen million?" Troy's father asked, his hands hanging limp at his sides.

"Where we *live*," she said. "Troy's friends. My job."

Troy's father froze, and the twisting vine of a smile grew across his face.

"Aha!" He paused. "Your job. Now I see. Your job, and maybe Seth Halloway's job, too?"

"No one said anything about Seth," Troy's mom argued, her back straightening.

"No." His father was quick. "No one *said* it, but there it is."

Troy's mom bit into her lower lip and glowered at his dad.

"I knew it," she said in barely a whisper. "Nothing ever changes. People never change. Please go."

"Tessa," his father said. "Don't do this. Think of Troy. Please. We don't have to like each other, but let's get along. This is just business. It's done."

"This is *not* just business," his mother said, waving her hands in the air. "This is my son. This is our life! Now go."

Troy's father pursed his lips. He gave Troy a sad look, mussed his hair, gripped one shoulder, and said, "It's all right, champ. She'll get over it."

"Don't bet on it," his mom said.

His father didn't even flinch; and as if Troy's mom hadn't spoken, he said, "This is all gonna work out, you'll see. You're my boy, right?"

"Of course," Troy said, liking the hand on his shoulder.

"Dad?" his father said with a smile and a wink.

"Of course, Dad," Troy said.

Troy's mom marched behind his dad to the door, with Troy trailing. When his father opened the Porsche's door, she said, "And don't tell him it's going to 'all work out' like you know something I don't. I don't care who promised what, *I'm* the one who has the final say. I'm going to look at what's best for Troy, and that's *not* New York."

CHAPTER FORTY-THREE

TROY'S MOM SLAMMED THE door and turned to him with an angry face.

"What?" Troy asked.

His mom's anger melted away. Her face fell, hopeless and pained.

"I am so sorry," she said, putting her arms around his neck and pulling him close.

Troy didn't know what to think, and certainly not what to say. Even though he let her hold him, he couldn't bring himself to hold her back.

Finally he asked, "Mom? Can I just go to practice?"

"Of course you can," she said. She sniffed and let him go. "Let me fix you something first, though. I'll call Seth to tell him you're coming. We didn't even know if you'd make it back."

"I almost didn't," Troy said.

"I can get John Marchiano to tell us what he thinks about all this," his mom said, digging through the refrigerator while he washed his hands in the kitchen sink. "How about spaghetti?"

"Great," he said, "but, Mom, shouldn't we really just do this deal with the Jets?"

His mom dumped a container of cooked noodles onto a plate and doused them with sauce and meatballs from a bowl before sticking it all inside the microwave. She dusted her hands and looked at him.

"New York?" she said, her lip curled with disgust. "You really want to move to that place?"

Troy shrugged. "It's the big time, Mom. The money is huge. New York is the center of the world."

"Don't listen to him," his mom said, shaking her head. "Don't let him poison you, Troy."

"No one's poisoning me, Mom," he said. "That's his job. He's supposed to get me the best deal. Shouldn't we think about this? Think if maybe it's really the best thing?"

"What do you want, Troy?" she asked softly.

"A lot of things," he said, his eyes finding the checkered tablecloth on the kitchen table. "I want to play in the NFL. I want to make a lot of money. I want to help the Falcons win the Super Bowl, but then I want to buy you a big new house and a fancy car."

"I don't care about all that," she said bitterly.

"Mom," he said, looking up. "You asked me what I wanted. I told you."

"I thought you and Gramps were the biggest Falcons fans on the planet," she said, her smile weak. "You think you could be okay with helping another team?"

"I know you don't want to hear this, Mom," Troy said, taking his seat, "but it's a business. Everyone says so, not just my dad. Seth Halloway. Mr. Langan. Everyone, Mom. It just is."

The microwave beeped, telling them his dinner had grown hot. She took it out with a pot holder and set it on the table along with a glass and a gallon jug of milk. She went to the bread box and took out some white bread and brought that over along with the butter dish before sitting down across from him and resting her face in her hands.

"You're right," she said. "Let's think about it. Go ahead, Troy. Eat."

He did eat, and when he finished, he changed into his practice gear and climbed into the VW bug. When they pulled into the Georgia Tech stadium, Troy couldn't help but remember the feeling of becoming a state champ only a few days ago right there, on the same field, under the same glow of lights.

From the parking lot, Troy could see that the all-star team wore a rainbow of colors. Each player was wearing his own junior league jersey. Troy saw a wide receiver and a running back from Valdosta, the team the Duluth Tigers had played against in the championship. One of the linemen wore the bright red of the Dunwoody Dragons, another Atlanta area team they'd defeated during the playoffs. There were lots of parents, too, since almost half of the players had to travel in from different regions all over the state.

As Troy trotted through the gates and out under the shadow of the goalposts, he heard Seth on the far end of the field calling his team together in the night air. The parents meandered toward the stands. Troy broke into a jog as Seth began passing out red pinnies to the defense and blue ones to the offense. When Troy pulled up to a stop at the back of the group, he looked expectantly at Seth.

Seth frowned at him and bent down into his bag, crumpling a blue pinnie and tossing it over the other players' heads for Troy to catch.

"You're late," Seth said.

Troy smiled, but Seth's mouth remained a flat line until he returned to his team speech, thanking them all for coming, especially those from far away who'd be staying at the nearby Courtyard Atlanta. Seth checked his clipboard and ran through his practice plan so everyone would know what to expect for the next few days, including a big team Thanksgiving dinner at the Ritz-Carlton downtown.

Seth hadn't finished speaking before Tate and Nathan sidled up to Troy and began pumping him with whispered questions about his absence from school and his reason for being late.

Troy only shook his head.

"I don't want to talk about it," he said. "My dad's working on a deal. That's all."

"Come on, man," Nathan said, leaning Troy's way but with his eyes fixed firmly on Seth. "You can't clam up on *us*. If it wasn't for us, Coach Krock would still be running the Falcons' defense and you'd be out on the street."

"He's right, you know," Tate said, chiming in.

Troy studied Seth's face, knowing that his mom must have let him in on the sudden trip to New York. The star linebacker had a smile plastered across his face like a piece of wallpaper, joyless and unmoving, but a smile all the same. Troy felt a pang of guilt.

"Don't you guys get it?" Troy asked, cranking his head around to glare at them. "I can't talk about it. I don't know what's going on."

"Sheesh, don't be so grumpy," Nathan said.

"Yeah, save it for the team from Florida," Tate said.

"Okay," Seth said, letting the clipboard drop to his side, "now, we're here to win this thing. I'm the head coach, and we'll do things my way. I know each one of you is a star, but forget that. For the next five days you guys are just a bunch of scrubs trying to win a starting job. Florida has been whipping our butts for the past five years. I watched the film. Our all-stars were just that, a bunch of stars floating around in space. Well, not this year. We're a machine. We're an army. There's no favorites, no sure starters. Each one of you will win or lose a starting job on this team in the next four days based on your performance.

"Now, I had to start out with something, so I've watched some film and made some quick evaluations. Let's just line up to get this thing started. I'll call out the starting defense and the starting offense. If you're a backup, stand behind your position and pay attention as we go through our base plays. Okay . . ."

Seth read off the defensive players, giving Nathan the nod as starting left tackle. Tate, everyone knew, was the kicker, because they didn't even have another. When Seth called out the offensive positions, quarterback was last. Troy buckled his helmet and started to jog for his spot behind the center and the rest of the linemen who stood waiting over the ball.

"Hey," Seth said, his voice cracking out over the field and echoing off the concrete stands, "Troy. Who said you were the starting quarterback?

"You're not."

CHAPTER FORTY-FOUR

TROY'S MOUTH FELL OPEN in disbelief. His cheeks burned with embarrassment as he slowly marched past the center and took up his position with the other second-stringers, behind the offense.

"You don't come late and start on this team," Seth said, loud enough for the entire team to hear it. "Later on we'll see how you throw with that bad finger. For now Glenn Twitchen will start out running the offense."

Troy stared hatefully at Seth and daydreamed about telling him right then and there that he'd signed a letter of intent with the Jets—*signed it*—for fifteen million dollars, and that he'd never be coming back to Atlanta, or the Falcons, and that Seth's own career would be finished. That's what he dreamed of as he stood there watching Glenn Twitchen, the quarterback from Athens, play his position.

When Seth sidled up to him as the starting offense ran a series of pass plays, Troy didn't even look at him.

"Hey," Seth said under his breath, "you hang in there. I need to prove to everyone that there aren't any favorites, bring this team together."

"I couldn't care less," Troy said bitterly.

"Troy," Seth said, "this is me. Relax. You do what you normally do and you'll be the starter on Saturday. You've got to have confidence."

"They wanted me to do *David Letterman* tonight," Troy said. "Did you know that? If I knew you were going to pull some junk like this, I sure wouldn't have busted my tail racing back here. I wouldn't have wasted my time with all this junk."

"Hey, Troy, easy."

"Easy?" Troy said. "Is this to get me back for Sunday? The difference is that you broke down. I'm fine. My finger . . ."

Troy wiggled the digit in disgust. "It'll be warm after three throws."

Seth stared at him and said, "Sunday? You think I blame you? You think I'd do that?"

Troy shrugged.

"Hey," Seth said, "buddy. All this talk about the big time with your new agent and the big contract and you being the salvation of football is going to your head. You're still a kid."

Seth stalked away, letting a sharp blast fly from his whistle before he barked at the running back for bobbling a handoff. Troy unsnapped his helmet, removed it, and turned to walk away. He'd nearly reached the fifty-yard line when he heard Seth shout from across the field, screaming at the top of his lungs.

"Hey, White!" Seth shouted. "Troy! You better get back here!"

Troy froze, then heard Tate's voice piping to him like a bird. "Troy! What are you doing? We need you!"

Troy hesitated, then kept going.

"Where do you think you're going, White?" Seth screamed in his ornery coaching voice.

Troy stopped and turned back, but only for a moment, to shout, "I'm going to New York!"

CHAPTER FORTY-FIVE

TROY SAW HIS MOM making a beeline from her seat in the stands for the gate leading from the field, and he forced air through his teeth. She met him with a scowl.

"What in the name of the good Lord are you doing?" she asked.

"Leaving," he said, trying to push past her.

"Oh, no," she said, grabbing his shoulder pad and yanking him around with surprising strength. "You march right back out there."

"This is bull!" Troy shouted, glaring up at her and twisting free from her grip. "I make him into an all-pro linebacker, but his stupid knees just can't take it. That's my fault? So he benches *me*? No way, Mom. I'm done with this. Border War. Who cares? I don't need the headache, and I sure don't need the scholarship money."

His mom's face got all pinched up.

"No," she said, "that's right. You've got all the money in the world if you want it now, right?"

"*We've* got all the money," Troy said, feeling less certain, his hand finding the edge of his thigh pad and tugging it into a more comfortable position.

"That's right," she said, "all we have to do is turn our backs on our friends, our home, the people we work with, our family, and we've got all the money in the world. That's a real nice trade-off, Troy. Really nice. I'm proud."

Troy hated her tone of voice, and he hated the look she was giving him. He looked out into the parking lot, wishing against all hope to see the orange Porsche speeding in from the street. He needed his father. His father understood. His mother was twisting things. She loved Seth; he knew that. That had to be what this was all about.

"Can I use your phone?" he asked.

"What?"

"Your phone," Troy said, holding out his hand. "I want to call my father."

"Your father?" she said, drawing out the syllables as if they were curse words.

"You don't have to drive me home," Troy said.

"You're talking crazy," she said. "Stop it."

"You stop it."

"Troy," she said, gritting her teeth.

"Then take me home," he said.

"No," she said, pointing. "You'll go back out there."

"Or what?" he asked.

His mom stepped closer to him and leaned forward so that their noses nearly touched. In a low, harsh tone she said, "If you think this is how it goes, you are sadly mistaken, mister. I *allowed* you to see your father. I gave him *permission* to represent us in this. I'm still your *mother. I* am your legal guardian. *I* call the shots. Your *father* abandoned you, and he abandoned me. I'm sorry. I know that hurts, but I'm not sure if he even knows the difference between what's right and what's wrong. I have my doubts."

Her voice dropped another notch and she said, "And if you think you and he have some power over me, I'll slap a restraining order on him so fast his head will spin. I'll call Seth Cole personally and tell him the deal's off no matter who promised what. *I'm* your mother. I can end this whole thing, send you to military school, and tell them no sports for you because you're to concentrate on your studies, so don't you ask me what *I'm* going to do, mister. Not ever again. Now, you *get* out there and *practice.*"

CHAPTER FORTY-SIX

TROY HUNG HIS HEAD.

He felt suddenly like a party balloon with a hole in its stem, the air hissing out in a steady stream.

"Okay," he said.

His mom nodded and marched for the gate leading out of the stadium.

"Where you going?" Troy asked.

"Business," she said without looking back. "You can get a ride home with Seth. I'll see you back at the house."

Troy started to protest, but she was moving fast, with her jaw set and her eyes squinted. He watched her go, then tugged his helmet on and slogged back out onto the field to take his place behind the offense, rejoining the other nonstarters.

"You get sick or something?" Seth asked, barking loud enough so everyone could hear and giving him an excuse so the whole team could put the incident behind them.

"Yes," Troy said.

"Better now?" Seth asked gruffly.

"Yes," Troy said.

Seth blasted his whistle, and the practice resumed.

When Troy finally got to run some plays, he did his best. He wasn't going to look like a big baby. If he had to stay, he'd stay and make the most of it. His finger didn't bother him much. If anything, the discomfort made him concentrate more on his form so that his passes zipped like bullets, clearly out-throwing Glenn Twitchen.

When practice ended, Troy stayed silent. He sat in the backseat of the H2, letting Nathan holler "Shotgun" and scramble into the front without a word of protest. Not even Tate could pull him free from his cloud of anger and frustration. Seth proved to be just as stubborn. He said nothing about the reason for Troy being second-string and kept equally silent on the drive home. At one point as they surged up Route 85, Tate put a hand on Troy's knee, squeezing it through the padding in his pants and offering a sympathetic smile. Still, Troy kept quiet except for the thanks he mumbled to Seth as he hopped down in front of his own house.

Tate, tireless to the end, said, "See you tomorrow, Troy."

Troy nodded and closed the door. Without looking

back, he turned and ran his hand along the smooth curve of his mom's VW, then climbed the stairs. He left his helmet and shoulder pads on the porch to dry out and went inside. His mom sat reading in her corner of the living room.

She looked up from her book and said, "Hello."

"Hi," Troy said, his voice low.

"Sulking won't make this any better," she said.

"I'm not," Troy said, even though he knew he was.

"Whatever," she said, dropping her nose back into her book.

Troy stood there for a moment in his sweaty practice pants and sleeveless Under Armour T-shirt before he sighed heavily and asked, "So, did you talk to him?"

"Who?" she said without looking up. "Drew?"

"My father," he said, delighted at the way her lip curled up at the word.

"No," she said, "I didn't need to."

"I thought you said you had business," he said.

"I do. I did," she said. "It's all set."

"But you're not going to tell me," Troy said, stepping into the living room with his hands on his hips and glaring at her.

"I can tell you," she said, looking up, with her voice as cheerful as the false smile on her face. "It's no big deal. I went and talked with Bob McDonough."

"Bob McDonough?" Troy said. "What's he got to do with any of this?"

Troy knew that Bob McDonough was the head of security for Mr. Langan. A former Secret Service agent who used to guard the president, Bob McDonough would sometimes help out with legal issues involving the team's players.

"He knows people," Troy's mom said, returning her attention to the book.

"What people?" Troy asked. "What are you talking about, Mom?"

His mom sighed and stood up, closing her book and slapping it gently against her leg. "I'm talking about people in the FBI, Troy. Law enforcement people who can look into someone's background."

"What are you talking about?" he asked, his stomach clenched.

"You see patterns on the football field," she said, "variables that your mind can put together like the pieces of a puzzle so that you know what's going to happen. Well, I see things, too. I know things—not about football, but about people. I see Drew and his fast car and this G Money character. I see the private jet, and I hear the smooth talk of someone who knows just what to say, how to push all the right buttons and get me to go along with his master plan, whatever that is. I see all this, and I have a sense of what's going to happen.

"You don't have to look at me like that. I'm not asking you to believe me because of what I'm sensing. That's okay. And I don't have to ask myself anymore either, what and why and who, or wonder if I'm right or wrong. Bob McDonough's friends at the FBI are going to find out."

"Find out what?" Troy asked, his voice raising in annoyance.

"What Drew is *really* up to," she said. "They have ways of looking into things that other people don't, ways of finding things out."

An alarm sounded in the back of Troy's mind.

"That's garbage!" he shouted. "You and Seth just want me to stay here so you can keep your jobs! You don't care about me, what I want! This is my chance at the big time. You can't just go get the FBI to start digging for dirt on my father. You can't!"

His mother patted his arm on her way past. She seemed unfazed by his rant. Heading to her bedroom, she said, "Oh, I already did."

CHAPTER FORTY-SEVEN

TROY DIDN'T SPEAK TO his mother the next morning, and she seemed okay with that. He found a seat alone on the school bus but didn't protest when Tate sat down next to him and Nathan took the seat behind them.

"So, we figured out what happened," Tate said, as cheerful as when he'd last seen her. "Seth told us."

"After he dropped you off last night," Nathan said, hanging over the back of the seat.

"And everything's going to be fine," Tate said.

Troy twisted up his lips and stared at the row of seats in front of him and the backs of the kids' heads as they jostled along.

"It's just because you were late," Nathan said, patting Troy's shoulder. "He had to set an example, with all the other kids not being from around here."

"He wants to make sure we win this thing," Tate said. "It's all coaching tactics, and you already know the offense better than anyone. So, you see? You don't have to be upset. We can just focus on winning this thing against Florida."

"And getting that fat cash," Nathan said, smacking a palm against his forehead and stroking his brush cut. "Sheesh! Ten grand."

"Well," Tate said after a few moments of silence, "this is good news, right?"

Troy sighed and said, "Not really. I don't care."

"Ha!" Nathan said, barking out his laughter. "What's the punch line? What do you mean you 'don't care'? Of course you care. It's ten grand. It's money for college. It's beating Florida for the first time in five years and impressing the college coaches. It's the big time."

"No, it's not," Troy said flatly. "That's not the big time. The big time is signing a huge contract with the New York Jets. The big time is having agents and lawyers who take care of things for you, being on TV, flying in private planes, swimming with the sharks. That's the big time, not some goofball all-star game."

Silence followed until the buzz of kids talking around them swallowed it up.

"I'm still waiting for the punch line here," Nathan said, poking Tate in the back of her neck. "What did I miss?"

Tate gripped the seat in front of her and faced

forward, her mouth set in a flat line.

"You didn't miss any punch line," she said. "He's serious."

"He's what?" Nathan said. "He can't be."

"Ten thousand dollars doesn't mean anything to him," she said, her voice bitter. "And he sure doesn't care about *us*."

"Right, 'cause it's all about you, Tate," Troy said. "You and Nathan and your scholarships, but what about me? This is a once-in-a-lifetime chance. I can set up me and my mom for good. This is the big time for real. It's New York, the center of the whole world."

"Great," Tate said, picking up her book bag and slipping back into the seat behind Troy and alongside Nathan.

"Fine," Troy said, spitting out the word.

"Good," Tate said, then banged the seat in front of them with her hand.

Troy jumped up the second the bus came to a stop in front of the school. He hurried inside without looking back, got the things from his locker, and hurried to homeroom. Halfway through first period, he told the teacher he didn't feel well. She told him to go see the nurse. Instead of the nurse's office, Troy headed for the pay phone down by the gym, sneaking through the halls with an eye out for monitors.

He took a quarter from his pocket and dialed his father's cell phone.

"Dad," he said, "you gotta get me out of here."

"Hi, Troy," his father said, sounding as if he was still in bed. "Out of where?"

"School," Troy said. "Atlanta. My mom. All of it."

The instant the words left his mouth, Troy regretted them. He knew he was being a hothead, something his mom sometimes accused him of being and something he knew to be true. It was all so confusing, the joy of finding the father he always wanted and the thrill of being with him and the things they did, but at the same time finding himself fighting with the people he knew and truly loved: his mom, Tate, Seth, and even Nathan.

His dad said, "You don't really mean that."

Troy felt relief, like peering over the dizzying edge of the outlook railing atop Stone Mountain and pulling back to feel the sturdy granite beneath his feet.

"No," he said. "You're right. I don't."

"Good," his father said. "I'm glad."

"But my mom is making a stink about me going to the Jets," he said. "I don't think she wants me to go to New York."

Troy heard his father breathing into the phone before he said, "When your mom realizes how good it is for you, she'll come around. Don't worry, Troy."

"I think Seth wants her to stay here," Troy said. "I think he wants me here, too. He needs me."

"His career is almost over, Troy," his father said. "He's a good man. He won't expect you to throw away your own chances just so he can hang on for a few more games."

The words his father spoke fell like seeds in Troy's mind, seeds that sprang into stalks of reason blooming full of kindness.

"You're right," Troy said.

"So, don't worry," his father said. "This will all work out."

"But she said she could stop me," Troy said, wanting to bring up the FBI but feeling too ashamed even to mention it, as if that would make it seem like he believed it was true.

"Relax," his father said. "If I know anything, it's how your mother thinks. Let her cool off. Don't push her. She's got a soft spot, and if you just don't push too hard, you can get right in there, and before you know it, she's on your side."

"She's talking about not letting me work for the Falcons, or anyone else," Troy said. "She's talking about sending me to military school. No football. No football genius. Just me being an average kid."

"She wouldn't do that, Troy," his father said, a sharp edge creeping into his voice. "The Jets are talking about five million dollars just for signing. Five million dollars! She's not crazy."

"She's not?" Troy said. "Well, no one told her that."

"Look, where are you now?"

"School," Troy said. "I don't feel great. I'm on my way

to the nurse, and I stopped to use the pay phone."

"I've got to get you a cell phone," his father said. "I should have done it already."

"Anyway," Troy said after a moment of silence.

"Yes," his father said, "anyway, you go see the nurse. I'll get this worked out with your mom. She'll see."

"Dad?" Troy said, the phone slick from the sweat of his grip.

"Yeah, Troy?"

"I trust you."

"And I trust you, too," his father said. "You're my boy. Don't worry. This will all work out."

"It will?" Troy said.

"You'll see."

Troy said good-bye, told the nurse he was feeling better, went back to class, and finished out the day.

What he saw when he got home wasn't anything good.

CHAPTER FORTY-EIGHT

BOB McDONOUGH STOOD TALL and slender, with close-cropped, graying hair and pale blue eyes that meant business. He stood talking to Troy's mom on the front porch. When they noticed Troy, they stopped talking. His mom gave Troy a look of concern and said they'd better go inside. Troy sat opposite Bob McDonough at the kitchen table while his mom flipped the tops off of three sodas, setting them out like pieces on a board.

"Bob," Troy's mom said, "would you please tell Troy what you learned."

Bob McDonough took a swig, and his eyes flickered from Troy's mom to Troy before he set down the bottle, licked his lips, and sucked in some air.

"Troy," he said, "you're an employee of the team, and it's my job to look into these kinds of things, whether someone is working a con game on one of our players or someone's trying to get inside information on the team for gambling. I admit that this is quite different, but you're an asset to the team."

"Only for the rest of this season," Troy said, jutting out his chin. "I'm going to the Jets next year."

"Yes, your mom told me about that," Bob McDonough said, casting a worried glance at Troy's mom, "but what I have to say may change all that."

"Because you want me to stay!" Troy said, pushing back his chair with a screech and jumping up.

"Troy!" his mother said. "Sit down. You don't talk to Mr. McDonough that way. You know better."

"I don't know what I know anymore," Troy said, then lowered his voice. "But I'm sorry. I didn't mean anything by it, Mr. McDonough; it's just that all this is so crazy."

"It'd be a lot for anyone," Bob McDonough said, "let alone a twelve-year-old boy. But that doesn't mean I can keep the truth from you, Troy."

"What truth?" Troy asked. "Why are you two looking like that?"

"Troy," Bob McDonough said, "your father, Drew Edinger, he's in very serious trouble with the law."

"What?" Troy asked, frightened by the look on Bob McDonough's face. "What trouble?"

CHAPTER FORTY-NINE

"YOUR FATHER IS MILLIONS of dollars in debt, Troy," Bob McDonough said. "He thinks you're his ticket out."

Troy remembered the man at G Money's card table who had referred to Troy as his dad's "ticket." He looked from Bob McDonough to his mom and back before he said, "That's not trouble with the law. People have money trouble. That's not a crime."

Bob McDonough shook his head slowly. "No, it's not, but when the fund he managed started to melt away, he took money from some very bad and dangerous people. He took the money that came from criminal activities and put it into legitimate real estate deals. It's called money laundering."

"Why? What are you talking about, laundering?" Troy asked.

"The money he got was dirty," Bob McDonough said, glancing at Troy's mom. "Money from drugs, gambling, extortion. Like I said, criminal activity."

"Even if it's true," Troy said, panic beginning to flood his mind, "he didn't do any of that stuff. No way. Never."

"No, he didn't," Troy's mom said, her voice soft, "but even taking that money the way he did and using it for those people is a crime. Troy?"

Troy opened his mouth but was too afraid to ask what, so nothing came out.

His mom looked at Bob McDonough, who nodded and said, "Your father is looking at about ten years in jail, Troy."

CHAPTER FIFTY

TROY BOLTED UP OUT of the chair, tipping it over this time. He ran out the front door. The pine branches scratched his arms and face as he batted blindly through the woods, heading in the general direction of the railroad tracks, not thinking or knowing where he wanted to end up. Behind him, he could hear his mother's cries to come back.

He kept going. When he broke into the open cut of the railroad bed, he leaped up onto the tracks and headed for the bridge. His mind swam in a hot soup of rage and disgrace and broken dreams. When his feet hit the metal trestle, he ran ten more strides and stopped in the middle. Below, the green snake of the Hooch slipped past. Jagged roots and rocks too stubborn to be swept away poked out from the red banks,

211

and the leafless trees stretched their fingertips across the expanse, leaving only a narrow column of blue sky above.

Troy had jumped into the Hooch before. Less than two months ago he'd taken the dangerous plunge, frustrated then about the father he never knew. Now he wished none of it had ever happened. What good was a father who would soon be in jail? And Troy knew what his mom and Bob McDonough were thinking. He'd seen it in their eyes, in their faces. They believed—and Troy couldn't help thinking it now himself—that the whole reason his father had even showed up was because of the money.

Troy gripped the lip of a slanted steel girder overhead. He leaned forward, out into the empty space, and lost his lunch in a stream that spun and floated until disappearing with a faint splat into the river below.

Troy wiped his mouth on a sleeve, then felt his stomach heave again. Nothing came out, but his insides twisted painfully all the same, and his choking noises drifted out across the steady water. Tears coursed down his cheeks, and he let them fall freely from his face without wiping them. The small dots of salty water fell like tiny bombs, lost from sight after only a few feet, gone as if they never were—and that's the way Troy liked it.

After a time he sat down and dangled his legs over the water. The sun slanted low across the treetops, painting them with yellow light. Troy thought about football practice and laughed out loud.

None of that mattered.

He sat for a long time with his mind mostly numb. The shadows deepened toward evening, and the river below turned dark enough to hide its movements. When Troy heard the sound of his mother calling his name, he sniffed and shifted his seat, wiping the last smudges of tears from his face. For ten minutes he listened as her calls grew closer and closer until he heard the rap of her feet on the steel bridge. She stopped calling, but Troy heard her all the same as she moved steadily closer and the final sound of her footfalls ended beside him.

"You can't keep running away, Troy," she said.

"I won't," he said, his voice, like his heart, empty.

"Bob McDonough wasn't finished. He had more to say."

"I don't want to hear it," Troy said. "I know everything. I know what you know, and I'm done trying to defend him. I've known all along that I've got this bad side to me, and I knew it never came from you."

"Oh, Troy," she said, sitting down beside him and snaking her arm around his shoulders, hugging him tight.

"I'm done crying about it," he said.

"Good," she said, her voice a whisper. "But it isn't completely hopeless, Troy. There's something you can do."

"Like what?" he said, his voice dull and disinterested.

"You can help your father," she said.

A small spark of hope glowed deep in a pit in his mind.

"What do you mean?"

"I mean," she said, "that the FBI wants your help. Mr. McDonough's friend said you could help them."

"Help them put my own dad in jail?" Troy asked, looking up at her and blinking in disbelief.

"I don't know if anything can keep him out of jail for certain, Troy," she said, "but the way I understand it is if you're willing to help, they'll take it into account."

"What's that mean, Mom?" he asked.

She sighed. "He could get ten years in jail. If you help them, maybe it's only one. Maybe he even gets off with probation. It's not him they really want."

"Who is it?"

"The people with G Money," his mom said. "They say he started hanging around with some mobsters from Eastern Europe to help his image in the rap world. I guess a lot of the rappers associate with criminal gangs. He did something different, not a street gang, but something just as dangerous. For some insane reason, I guess it helps a person in the music business to have a bunch of crooks for friends. It's those people who gave Drew the dirty money."

"I saw them," Troy said. "Outside G Money's. Playing poker by the pool. They looked mean."

"They are," his mom said. "Very."

"But how can I help?" Troy asked.

"Well," she said, "if you'll come back to the house, that's what we're both about to find out."

"Why?" Troy asked. "Who's at the house."

"The FBI."

CHAPTER FIFTY-ONE

TROY SAW HIS GRAMPS'S pickup in the dirt patch along with a navy sedan in the deepening shadows beneath the pine trees. Gramps met them at the door.

"Gramps?" Troy said. "What are you doing here?"

"Just providing counsel," Gramps said, smiling at Troy's mom. "Someone thinks I'm not only old but wise, too."

Gramps gave Troy's shoulders a squeeze before leading them into the kitchen. Bob McDonough sat at the kitchen table with two other men, both with short hair and wearing crisp, dark suits. Troy's mom pointed to a chair for him to sit in. She positioned herself by the sink, leaning back against the counter with her arms folded. Gramps took a stool from the corner and sat down on it next to her.

Bob McDonough introduced the men in suits as Agent Kerns and Agent Williams, with Williams having the friendlier-looking face of the two.

It was Williams who said, "Troy, do you know what kind of trouble your father is in?"

"I think so," Troy said.

The agent nodded and said, "And did your mom tell you that if you help us, we'll do everything we can to minimize the time he spends in jail?"

"She said one year instead of ten," Troy said, looking hard into the agent's eyes. "Or maybe he might not even go."

"Yes," Williams said, "that's right. Now, we can't promise anything specific other than that whatever would have happened, it'll be a lot better for him with this deal. We'll tell the judge that he helped us through you. And it is possible he won't go to jail at all. Maybe just lose his license to practice law and get probation."

"Can't you just leave him alone completely if I help you?" Troy asked, his voice desperate.

It was Agent Kerns who scowled and shook his head.

"Not completely, Troy," Agent Williams said. "I'm sorry."

"What if I don't help?" Troy said, raising his chin.

"We can't make you," Agent Williams said, glancing

at Troy's mom and Gramps, then at Bob McDonough. "But like I told your mom, I think you'd regret it, Troy. No one wants his father in jail, and that's where he's headed right now. We aren't going away. We'll get these people. It may take years, but sooner or later they'll make a mistake. They've made one right now, but we can't take advantage of it without your help."

"Let's talk about what it is you want him to do," Troy's mom said. "He's not doing anything dangerous. No way. I told you all that."

"And we promised it wouldn't be," Agent Williams said. "No one will suspect a thing."

From his pocket, the agent removed a quarter. He flipped it in the air for everyone to see, then caught it and slapped it down into his palm. "All he has to do is drop this down behind a piece of furniture or slip it into the cushions on the zebra couch in G Money's living room. Not that anything could happen, but if it does, we'll be listening the whole time. We're set up next door, and we can be inside in a matter of seconds if Troy needs us."

"You saw the couch?" Troy asked. "Then how come you didn't do it yourselves?"

"We see the couch with spotting scopes and heat-sensing equipment from the neighbor's roof," Agent Kerns said in a stern voice. "That couch is where Luther Tolsky does all his business. They come and go and we can see them, but we can't hear anything. We get a listening device in that room and we can nail this guy good."

"Wait a minute," Troy said. "Luther Tolsky? The big, scary-looking guy? Bald with a thick black beard and a tattoo on his neck?"

Agent Williams narrowed his eyes at Troy and said, "You've seen him, right?"

"At the dome with G Money and my dad," Troy said, "and at G Money's pool, playing cards."

"That's our target, a very bad man," Agent Williams said, "but also a very smart man. He changes the place he conducts business every week. We never know where he'll be. He has a lot of contacts: people he can trust or people too afraid to tell him no. By the time we get the court orders for the wiretaps in place and figure out a way to get someone inside to plant one of these quarters, he's already moved on.

"But with your dad staying there, this will be easy."

"What if he can't get into the living room?" Troy's gramps asked.

"Look, we're not asking for guarantees," Agent Williams said. "We just want Troy to try. Nothing can happen. Look at this thing. It's a quarter."

The agent handed it to Troy's mom. She turned it over in her hand and passed it to Gramps before she asked, "What do you think, Dad?"

Gramps rolled the coin around with his fingers, then held it out away from him to see it better before he said, "Dropping this thing, I can't see how it could hurt, Tessa."

"No," the agent said, "it can't, but it could help. It could help us, and help his dad stay out of jail."

Troy's mom looked at Gramps. He sighed, gave the quarter back to Agent Williams, and nodded. In a quiet voice he said, "If he doesn't do it, Tessa, I'm afraid Troy will always look back on this moment and regret it. Jail is a horrible thing, and I think, good or bad, Troy loves his father. You know that."

"I wish his father loved him back as much," Troy's mom said.

Troy hung his head.

Softly his mom said, "I shouldn't have said that, Troy. I'm sorry."

Troy shrugged and said, "It's okay. I understand. I still want to help him, Mom. I'm not afraid, and maybe he's not as bad as they think. That's possible, right?"

Troy looked at the agents. Kerns's lips disappeared into the flat slit of his mouth.

Williams tilted his head and said, "Well, sometimes strange things happen; but in this business, it usually turns out just the way you think it will."

Everyone sat quiet for what seemed like a long time before, in a soft and serious voice, Troy's mom asked,

"If we agree to this, Agent Williams, when would you want him to do it?"

The agents looked at each other, and it was Kerns who answered.

"Right now. Tonight."

CHAPTER FIFTY-TWO

"**WHEN WE SAW YOU** at G Money's the other night," Agent Williams said, "you just appeared out of nowhere. How did you get there?"

Troy bit his lip and raised his eyes toward his mom. She furrowed her eyebrows and said, "Wait a minute. He rode there with Drew last night, right?"

"No," Agent Williams said, "he just showed up on his own Sunday night."

Troy winced and studied the checkered tablecloth.

"Sunday night," his mom said, her voice as flat as a pancake. "Interesting."

His mom sighed loudly before adding, "Dad, I don't know what I'm going to do with him."

Troy snuck a look at his gramps, who said, "I know what you do. You just love the boy. He wants a father.

He's wanted that for a long time. Everyone wants that, Tessa, and it's hard for those of us who've had a father to know what it's like not to. Let it go, darlin'. He's a good kid."

"Okay, Dad," she said. "You're right."

"Most times." He grinned.

"So," Troy's mom said, "how did you get there, Troy?"

"The wall," Troy said under his breath. "And Gramps's ladder."

"Great."

"Tessa," Gramps warned.

"Okay." Troy heard the sound of surrender in her voice.

"So, that's what we need you to do this time, too," Agent Williams said. "We can't risk having anyone see you being dropped off down the street. You just go in the same way you did before, only this time you'll be carrying our quarter.

"Now, do you have a reason to go see your dad?"

Troy knit his brow and said, "I guess the deal we agreed to, and my mom wanting to back out of it. I mean, it's something that *might* make me want to go see him. Not that I was going to do that."

Troy stole a look at his mom, who flashed him a mildly disgusted look.

"Perfect," Agent Williams said. "That's what you tell him. That will keep them all off guard, and I won't be surprised if this whole contract thing isn't part of their business."

"What?" Troy said.

"This contract," Agent Williams said, "how fast he put it together. I think Drew Edinger is under a lot of pressure. Your contract might be just what he needs to turn down the heat."

"Why would my contract do that?" Troy asked.

"The money, Troy," Agent Williams said. "Anything's possible, but I think he's planning on taking it for himself."

"What?" Troy said with even more disbelief. "Even if he *wanted* to, how could he do that?"

CHAPTER FIFTY-THREE

"HE'S YOUR LAWYER," BOB McDonough said with a solemn face. "He can do a lot of things."

"Not take my money," Troy said, a gust of laughter escaping him in disbelief. "You can't take someone's money."

"It happens all the time," Agent Williams said, casting a glance at Troy's mom. "People trust their lawyers. They sign what's put in front of them without reading the fine print, and before you know it . . ."

"I signed something that agreed he could act as Troy's agent," Troy's mom said, staring at her own hands. "But . . . you're right, I didn't read it very carefully."

"Don't worry," Agent Williams said. "We get this bug planted in that living room, and even if they try something we'll get the money back."

Troy wanted to say that he didn't care about the money, if that was the case, because as disgusted and embarrassed as he was, he still had no wish to destroy his father and no wish to prove that Drew was as bad as Troy's mother believed. Instead, he looked at his gramps, who sometimes had the amazing ability to know Troy's thoughts as well as he knew them himself.

"The money isn't the most important thing," Gramps said, his bright blue eyes locked on Troy's. "Let's focus on the task at hand. Money has a funny way of taking care of itself, and if that's what you're really after—money—you'll never have enough of it anyway. It's like a dog chasing its tail."

"Good," Agent Williams said, "then we all agree? We have your cooperation?"

"Troy?" his mom said. "You're sure?"

"Yes, Mom."

"Dad?" she asked.

"Yes."

"So, we're in," Troy's mom said.

"Our people are already set up," Agent Williams said. "If you're ready, so are we."

"You just want me to take the ladder and climb the wall?" Troy asked.

"Whatever you did Sunday night," Agent Williams said, "do the same thing this evening."

Troy looked out the window and saw that the shadows had grown deeper still. It was truly dusk; the sun had gone down, and only its memory and a final glow remained in the west.

"Let me make him something to eat first," Troy's mom said, sounding so much like a mom that Troy had to smile.

The agents looked at each other. Bob McDonough held up his hands in surrender, and the three men stood up from the table.

"We'll look for you in about an hour," Agent Williams said as they moved toward the door. "And Troy? If you don't get the opportunity to drop it in or near the zebra couch, don't worry. We might get another chance. The thing we don't want to do is let Luther Tolsky know what we're trying to do. That could drive him so deep into cover that it would ruin all the progress we've made. You understand, right?"

"Yes," Troy said. "Absolutely."

Agent Williams held out the quarter, pinched between his thumb and forefinger. Even with a knotted stomach Troy held out his hand, and the agent dropped the coin into his palm.

"Spend it wisely," Agent Williams said.

"Don't worry," Troy said in a whisper. "I will."

CHAPTER FIFTY-FOUR

TROY'S MOM WHIPPED UP macaroni and cheese for him and Gramps, chattering the whole time about the Ritz-Carlton Thanksgiving dinner while Troy and Gramps sat at the table with bottles of Coke, studying their shapes. Troy wasn't all that hungry, but he did his best because his mom was watching. Halfway through the meal, he remembered his football all-star team.

"Will you call Seth and tell him I'm not coming?" Troy asked.

"Maybe you should," his mom said. "No, that's not right. I'll do it. He won't ask questions if I do it."

"It's not like he's even starting me," Troy said.

"Troy," she said, "I spoke with Seth today about that. He said he had to do what he did because you showed up late. If you do what everyone knows you can do, and if you're healthy, you'll start."

"But now I'm missing a practice," Troy said. "Not that I care."

"So let's not think about it," his mom said. "But I will tell him. He's still your coach."

"Seth will understand," Gramps said, "and I bet you get to play in that game anyway."

Gramps held out his bottle to toast. Troy tapped the mouth of his bottle against Gramps's and took a slug of soda before finishing off the macaroni and cheese his mom had spooned onto his plate.

After dinner Troy helped clean up before his mom said, "Okay. So, you ready?"

Troy nodded, accepting the jeans jacket she took out of the coat closet before opening the front door. His mom gave Gramps a worried look and asked, "You sure, Dad?"

"He'll be fine," Gramps said, touching her cheek with the back of his fingers. "I wouldn't let him if I didn't know it. You know that, right?"

"Here," Troy's mom said, ducking back into the kitchen and returning with her cell phone. "Take this, Troy."

"Mom," he said, pointing to the quarter in his pocket, "they can hear everything. I'll be fine."

"Just take it, sweetheart," she said.

The look on her face made him slip the phone into his pocket.

"Well," Troy said, suddenly nervous but forcing a smile, "here I go."

He didn't close the door behind him, and he knew they stood there watching through the screen as he crossed the patch and hoisted the ladder on to his shoulders. He felt their concern as he disappeared into the pinewoods, heading for the railroad tracks and the wall beyond. When he emerged onto the railroad bed, the sky had gone from a pale, dying light to a deep purple bruise. He had to watch carefully where he stepped as he made his way closer to the wall.

It took some effort to get the ladder standing on its end and propped up against the wall, but his sweat dried quickly in the cool, crisp air. The trees crowded in on him with a pitch-black gloom. He put one hand on the cold, ribbed surface of a ladder rung and raised one foot.

The snap of a twig behind him made Troy gasp, jump, and spin around.

A cry got caught in his throat and he choked it back, terrified of making himself known. His fingers searched past his mom's cell phone for the quarter in his pocket. He prayed that the FBI agents were already listening.

"Gramps?" he whispered. "Mom?"

A small breeze sighed in the treetops above. Troy felt the current of panic racing through his veins with hot thoughts about criminal gangsters. His ears strained for more information. Then his body made the decision to run—not home, but up the ladder. He'd get over the wall as quickly as he could.

Troy turned and gripped the rungs, his feet scampering up. He'd nearly reached the top of the wall when he felt a hand rise up from the darkness below and grab his foot.

CHAPTER FIFTY-FIVE

TROY KICKED AND THRASHED, but the hand held tight.

"Hey!" came a shout from below.

Troy stopped kicking and said, "Tate?"

"Take it easy," she said in a hissing whisper.

"Are you nuts?" he said, letting go of the ladder rungs and dropping to the ground. He stuck his face into hers so that he could just make out her features in the dark. "You scared the heck out of me."

"Sorry," Tate said in a loud whisper. "I was trying to keep quiet. I saw you go across the tracks with this ladder practically from my house, and I followed you. What are you doing here?"

"What are *you* doing, Tate?" he asked, whispering himself now. "You've got football practice."

"So do you," she said, poking him in the chest with

a finger, her voice still hushed. "I'm just the kicker. We need you if we're going to win this thing on Saturday. When Seth told us you weren't coming to practice, I hopped right out of his truck and told them to go without me."

"Well," Troy said, touching the coin in his pocket, "I can't tell you what I'm doing."

"Okay," Tate said, nodding as if she wasn't surprised. "I'll come with you."

"You *can't*," he said.

"You look like you're scared," she said. "Your face is as pale as a ghost's."

"I'm *not* scared, Tate," he said, growling. "Now leave me alone, will you? I've got to do something important, and I can't talk about it, okay?"

Tate stepped back from him, and without whispering at all she asked, "We're still friends, though, right?"

"Of course," he said, letting his head sag before holding it up straight. "We're always friends, Tate. You know that. But I have to go."

"Okay," Tate said, nodding at the wall. "I'm sure it's about your dad."

Tate peered at him through the dark, but Troy said nothing.

"I understand, Troy," she said, sounding a bit sad. "I'll be at my house if you need me. For anything."

"Thank you, Tate," he said, then turned and climbed back up the ladder, pulling it up behind him so that he could use it to climb down the other side.

When he finished lowering it, he turned to say good-bye, but Tate had already disappeared.

"Bye," he said, so softly it was swallowed by the breeze. Then he scrambled down the ladder and set off for G Money's mansion.

CHAPTER FIFTY-SIX

THE SECURITY GUARDS AT the gate to G Money's driveway told him to leave. Troy pointed through the metal bars at his father's orange Porsche and told them he'd already been inside. They went through the same routine with their radios, and the gates buzzed and swung slowly open. One of the guards walked him up the curved drive and passed him off to one of the guards he recognized at the door.

"You're like gum on a shoe, kid," the house guard said as Troy followed him into the hall, past the enormous painting of G Money and into the very room where Troy needed to be.

"Your dad's coming," the guard said, leaving him alone.

Only the weak light coming in from the pool area

and two dim floor lamps lit the room. Troy headed straight for the zebra couch, which sat facing the big glass windows on the edge of a bearskin rug. His heart thumped up into his throat. He felt around the phone and pinched the quarter, his hand still deep in his pocket as he rounded the couch and gasped.

Luther Tolsky was lying sprawled out along the length of the black-and-white couch like a beached whale. The enormous man's fingers were intertwined and rested in the center of his chest. His eyes shot open. They widened, and he scowled at Troy through his rimless glasses.

"What are you doing here?" Luther Tolsky asked in an unfriendly rumble, the pink opening of his mouth flashing white teeth from its nest of black fur.

Troy snatched his hand out of his pocket, leaving the quarter behind.

"Nothing," he said, instantly aware that his answer wasn't good enough. "My dad. I'm meeting him."

Luther's face softened just a bit. "Yeah, you got the big money coming in, little man, don't you?"

"I think."

"You know," Luther said, scowling again. "Don't be a little daisy. You like daisies?"

"No," Troy said.

"No one does," Luther said. "Pretty little flowers that smell like junk. Say what you think. Think what you say."

Troy stood, frozen and scared.

Luther stared, waiting, then said, "So? You got the big money?"

"Yes."

White teeth flashed from the middle of Luther's thick beard. "That's a good boy. You do have it coming in. I heard about it. *Big* money. There is nothing wrong with money."

Troy just stood.

Luther sat up and scratched his beard, then flipped open his cell phone, dialed, and put it to his ear. Troy looked down at him, his eyes drawn to the tattered ear. One tail of Luther's silk shirt had escaped from his pants. The gold chain on his chest, resting in its bed of hair, glowed in the dull light from the pool. In Luther's eyes, Troy saw evil and death and the cunning of a warlock who could read your mind.

"Drew," Luther said, barking Troy's father's name, "you coming to meet your little man or no? Little Daisy woke me up from my nap. Come get the boy. In the zoo room. I got people coming from New York and that man from the Cayman Islands, and they won't want to see a kid."

Luther snapped the phone shut and looked around before he said, "Looks like a zoo in here, right?"

Troy nodded, glancing around at the animal skins laid out on the floor and stretched tight over the sofas, chairs, and footstools. Relief flooded his mind when his father appeared through a doorway on the far side of the enormous room, walking and laughing with G Money. Luther looked over his shoulder and nodded at Troy's dad and the famous rap star, then offered up a greeting that was little more than a grunt.

Troy's dad seemed to avoid eye contact with the grumpy big man. Instead, he gave Troy a wink and a clap on the back.

"Hey, partner," he said. "How's it feel to be a millionaire? G Money, my boy is in the big time."

"I hear you," G Money said, holding out a fist for Troy to bump. "What it is. New York is all that. You two gonna love the Big Apple."

"Hey!" Luther shouted. "Little man. You got any money now?"

Troy looked up at the enormous, scary man and blinked. Troy's father shot him a worried look, as if Luther were a fifteen-foot alligator loose from his pen. Troy waited for his father to save him, but no one said anything, and Luther's stare seemed to burn hotter by the second.

"What do you mean?" Troy said in a broken croak.

"Money," Luther said in disgust. "You know what that is, right?"

Troy nodded.

"How much money you got?" Luther asked.

Troy shrugged and shook his head, scared and unknowing.

"In your pocket," Luther said, slow and mean, dipping his chin toward the pocket where Troy held the FBI's quarter. "How much money you got in there? Go on. Dig in.

"Let me see."

CHAPTER FIFTY-SEVEN

TROY SLIPPED HIS FINGERS into the pocket.

He looked at his father. Drew gave him an odd half smile and tilted his head. Troy wondered if his father would keep him alive long enough for the FBI to get there in time, *if* they were listening.

His fingers closed around the cool metal disk and, hesitantly, he removed it from his pocket.

"Open your hand," Luther grumbled.

Troy's fingers slowly spread. The quarter gleamed up at them.

Luther began to laugh.

It started in low, then grew to a mad cackle.

"Twenty-five cents!" Luther hooted. "Look at your boy, Drew. Your little man is some kind of player, right?

240

Five million in the pipeline, and he's got a *quarter* in his pocket."

Troy's father joined in the laughter, as did G Money; soon Troy realized it was real laughter, all of it. He broke out in a relieved laugh of his own, looking from one face to another. When it died down, Luther wiped a tear from the corner of one dark and red-rimmed eye and sniffed. Then from his own pocket he removed a fat wad of hundred-dollar bills.

"This is how you carry your money, little man, in a roll," Luther said, "if you're lucky enough to have this much. But you are lucky, right? Lucky for your dad, that's for sure. Lucky like a rabbit's foot."

Troy's father hesitated, then said, "I was lucky to find him."

Luther snorted, stuffed the roll of cash back into his pocket, and looked at G Money, who shrugged as though afraid to take a side.

"That and more," Luther said to Troy's dad with a scowl before he glanced at his watch. "All right. I got this meeting in two minutes, so you take this little family reunion someplace else."

Troy studied G Money, thinking that since it was his house, he'd have something to say about who would go where. Troy was wrong. G Money listened to the big thug like a schoolboy hoping to get out of the principal's office. The rapper flicked his chin, signaling Troy and his dad to follow him. Even though he hadn't completed his mission, Troy could only feel relief at the thought of being free from the horrible gaze of Luther Tolsky.

They hadn't taken two steps before a guard barged in from the entrance and said, "Hey, G Money. We got another kid now."

"What?" G Money said, rumpling his face.

That's when the guard reached behind him, grabbed hold of a collar, and shoved Tate into the big room.

CHAPTER FIFTY-EIGHT

LUTHER'S PINK GRIN APPEARED in the midst of his beard, G Money flashed his own gold grille, and Troy's dad joined in.

"Little man is some kind of Romeo," Luther said. "Come on in here, Juliet."

Tate folded her arms across her chest and scowled at them all.

"Tate," Troy said in disbelief, "what are you doing?"

"Making sure you're all right," she said, glaring at him like the whole thing was his fault.

"I'm fine," Troy said.

"Right," she said, drawing out the word to show her disbelief.

"You want me to bounce her on out of here, G?" the guard asked.

"You remember Tate, G Money?" Troy quickly said. "My friend from the Falcons game. Down on the field?"

"You can't take the little man's shorty," Luther said, laughing.

With the men's attention on Tate, Troy realized in a flash that he had a chance to do what he'd come for. The thought of his father going to jail forced his hand into his pocket. He clutched his mom's cell phone with the quarter pressed tight to its side. When he removed the items, he kept his eyes on the men and let the quarter slip from his hand so that it fell to the bearskin rug with the faintest thump.

"Oh, Troy," Tate said, obviously embarrassed by the men's attention and wanting to get out from under it any way she could.

"I think maybe you just dropped a quarter or something."

CHAPTER FIFTY-NINE

TATE POINTED AT THE floor, and the men's eyes all followed its direction, looking at Troy's feet. Troy made a show of looking down himself and bent to scoop the money out of the rug, holding it up in his free hand.

"Wow," he said, "yeah. Got it. Thanks, Tate."

Troy's face warmed as he tucked the quarter back into his pocket.

"Okay, scat," Luther said, jabbing his thumb toward the door as he stepped to a side table and poured himself what looked like a whiskey to Troy.

"Come on," Troy's dad said, motioning to them. "Let's go sit by the pool and we can talk."

"Yeah," Luther said, raising his drink, "and I'll call you when I need you, Drew. That Cayman Islands thing, right?"

"Right," Troy's dad said. "Sure."

As they crossed the big room for the doors, Troy heard the sound of men arriving at the front door, laughter, greetings, and the slap of handshakes.

When they'd passed through the sliding doors and were alongside the pool, Troy asked, "What's that Cayman Islands thing all about?"

His father flinched but then quickly gave Troy a smile and a wink and said, "Just business."

"With that guy?" Troy asked.

"He's G Money's friend," Troy's dad said, lowering his voice. "If G Money wants to do something with him, I've got to stay on top of the deal. I'm the lawyer."

"What kind of a deal is it?" Troy asked, hoping against hope that his father would come up with something to prove the FBI agents wrong.

"Nothing you'd understand, Troy," his dad said. "Stop asking questions, will you? Why'd you come over here anyway? Did you climb over the wall?"

"Yeah," Troy said. "Tired of fighting with my mom, I guess."

"I get it," his dad said, showing them to seats around the table on the terrace where the men had played cards. "Let me get you two something to drink. Coke? Grape soda? Mountain Dew?"

"Orange soda if you have it," Tate said.

"Coke," said Troy.

The instant his dad disappeared down the shrub-lined path heading for G Money's bar by the end of the pool, Troy said, "Tate, are you kidding? What the heck are you even *doing* here? Do you know what you just did with that quarter?"

Tate gave him a worried look and shrugged. "Saved you twenty-five cents?"

"It's the whole reason I'm *here*," Troy said in an urgent whisper that he also used to quickly tell her the story about the FBI.

By the time he finished, Tate's forehead was wrinkled with concern.

"These people are, like, criminals?" Tate asked.

"I guess they are."

"But if you help, then they'll help your dad?"

"Yes."

"We have to get that thing back in there," she said as if speaking to herself.

"How?" Troy said, huffing. "I can't just walk back in there. That guy's scary. He's dangerous; that's what the FBI said. You see the way he looks at me?"

"No, you can't," Tate said, distracted by her thoughts until she looked up at him. "But *I* can."

"*You* can?" Troy asked. "How?"

CHAPTER SIXTY

TATE'S EYES FLASHED IN the direction of the bar. She leaned forward and said, "Your dad's coming. Give it to me, quick."

"How, Tate?"

She growled at him and said, "When a girl's gotta go, a girl's gotta go; now *give* me that."

Troy reached in his pocket, removed the quarter, and held it out across the table. He hesitated, looking into Tate's dark brown eyes. He dropped the coin into her hand. She snapped her hand shut and jumped up, brushing past Troy's dad and his drinks.

"Where you going, Tate?" Troy's dad asked.

"The facilities," Tate said.

Troy's dad looked away and nodded, and Troy thought that she just might be right. He knew that whenever a girl he'd been around mentioned anything having to do with the bathroom, the mind of every guy within earshot would go blank. It was like a stun gun, rendering them useless.

From his spot, Troy could see Tate working her way through the maze of shrubbery, past the pool. She was headed right for the sliding doors of the great room, even though the small cluster of men around the zebra couch was clear to see.

"She's a fireball," Troy's dad said, sitting beside him and plunking down the sodas on the big round table.

His dad's appreciation of Tate only made Troy sad.

"Dad?" Troy said.

"Yeah? Oh, wait," his father said, raising his soda can. "Here's to five million dollars. Right?"

Troy clinked his can against his father's and took a swig.

"What'd you want to tell me?" his father asked.

"If I could help you," Troy said, "I would, you know."

His father's face twisted up for an instant as if he might cry, but then the pained look was gone. And when his father grinned hard at him and winked, Troy wasn't sure it had ever happened. Maybe he'd imagined it.

"I know you would," his father said, clapping his shoulder. "I'm your dad. I don't doubt it. You're a good kid, Troy."

"And I'd never do anything to hurt you, Dad," Troy

said, looking away because he didn't trust his own emotions to stay in check the way his father's had.

"Is there something you've got to tell me, Troy?" his father asked. "You're not going to ask me to back out of the deal? It's too late for that, Troy."

Troy sighed and said, "No, it's a great deal."

"It sure is. So, we're good?" his father said, raising his can again as if they were toasting all over.

"Good," Troy said, and he dared a peek at the big window where he could clearly see Tate standing inside the zoo room with her back to him. The group of suspicious-looking men stared at her, astonished. Tate's arms flew about with her hands flitting through the air to assist in the telling of what Troy knew must be some crazy story.

Troy cleared his throat, looked into his father's eyes, and said, "I just wanted to see you. It's still pretty cool for me to just see you. I thought about you for a long time."

His father's grin went slack, and in a sad way he said, "And I've thought about you, Troy."

Troy's insides froze.

"But," he said, "I . . . thought you didn't know about me?"

CHAPTER SIXTY-ONE

THE SMILE FLASHED BACK onto his father's face instantly.

"The *idea* of you," his father said, "of having a son. I told you. I always wanted that. That's all I meant, not that I knew *you* really existed. I thought a lot about having a *son*. Just the idea."

"Oh," Troy said.

Tate appeared, marching up onto the terrace and crossing her arms over her chest.

"How you two doing?" she asked, grabbing her soda from the table, cracking open the can with a hiss, and swigging some down. As she drank, she flashed a thumbs-up behind her back, a signal only Troy could see, that told him she'd done her job.

"Great," Troy's dad said, answering Tate's question. "One of those father-and-son talks."

"You want me to let you guys talk?" Tate asked. "I can."

"No, that's okay, Tate," Troy said. "We've got to get back anyway."

"You don't want to finish your sodas?" his dad asked.

"We can take them," Troy said, standing. "I know you've got things going on."

As if on cue, the glass doors slid open and someone Troy had never seen before, with tan skin and a pencil-thin mustache, stepped out onto the deck and shouted, "Edinger! We need you! The big man does!"

He disappeared back inside, and one of the guards from the front of the house came out, heading their way. Troy's dad gave him a sheepish look.

"Well," his dad said, "you're right about the business part of it. Okay, well, you two get back home. And, Troy, if I don't see you tomorrow, it's because your mom is being a crank and I might have to shoot back to Chicago quick to take care of some things, but don't worry. Everything will smooth out soon, and we'll be hanging out again. I'm not only your dad; I'm your lawyer. You can't go wrong."

Troy thought it sounded like his dad was trying to sell him a car, but he let Drew hug him before they stepped apart. The guard muttered to them that Luther had asked him to escort the kids to the front gate. Troy and Tate said good-bye to Troy's dad and followed the guard down a path that took them around the house instead of through it. When they reached the driveway, Troy looked back at the huge white mansion to see that two white stretch limos now waited in the glow of the lights right in front of the grand front steps leading to the door.

When the gates hummed open, Troy took Tate's arm and hurried her through. He said thanks to the guard, using all his determination not to break out into a full sprint and run away as fast as his legs would take him.

"*I did it*," Tate said before they had even rounded the corner.

"*Shhhh!*" Troy said, clutching her arm as the gates swung slowly closed.

"You're hurting me," she said under her breath.

"Don't run," he said, glancing back as they rounded the corner beneath the glow of a street lamp. "Nothing suspicious."

"When can we?" Tate said as they reached the next stop sign and a bit of darkness, where they could take another turn.

Just then Troy glanced back again and saw a man beneath the streetlight, wearing a dark suit and holding a radio in one hand, sprinting their way.

"Now!" Troy said, and they took off.

CHAPTER SIXTY-TWO

TROY TOOK A RIGHT at the next stop sign and bolted in between a grassy stretch separating two big homes. Even in the dark he knew that the secret path he'd followed through the trees and underbrush behind the homes to get to Seth's place wasn't far. Tate kept up, but Troy could feel that the shadowy man—who remained frighteningly silent—was gaining on them. On a hunch, Troy broke through a line of shrubs, but when he came out the other side, he slammed full speed into a chain-link fence.

He recovered quickly and sprinted up the fence line and into a stand of pine trees, where the glow of a nearby pool let him see. The bushes swished behind him, and he heard the man crash into the fence just as he had. The undergrowth got suddenly thick and dark;

254

Troy grabbed Tate by the arm and pulled her straight into it with him, the branches and brambles whipping their faces and cutting their hands.

Then it ended. They broke free into a swath of grass that bordered the concrete wall surrounding Cotton Wood. Troy sensed the spot and took a hard right. When he glanced back, he saw nothing of the man's dark shape. With his lungs on fire, he put his head down and ran even faster. The ladder wasn't too far.

When they reached it, Troy had to use all his inner strength and every lesson his mom had taught him not to just scramble up and drop down over the other side. Instead, the noble side of him won out, and he handed Tate up the ladder so she could climb up to the top of the wall. When she did, she looked down the way they'd come, and a muffled whine escaped her.

"Troy," she said, "hurry! He's coming!"

CHAPTER SIXTY-THREE

TROY NEVER LOOKED BACK; he bolted up the ladder, spun, and grabbed it. The shadowy man closed in. Full speed he ran. The man grunted something that sounded like "ate." The sound sent a shiver through Troy.

"Stop!" the man shouted in a deep, husky voice.

Troy heaved the ladder up and over the wall and sent it crashing down the other side. Tate already hung from the edge of the wall by her fingertips, and she dropped down beside the ladder. Troy crouched down, too, aware of the man closing in. He gripped the rim of the wall as Tate had, then dropped to the ground with a thud.

Together they looked up at the top of the wall, listening silently as the man on the other side grunted for them to come back and scraped at the concrete as he leaped over and over again for the top of the wall, straining for a grip on its peak so he could finish the chase.

"Let's go," Troy said, not giving one hoot about the ladder lying in the brush.

He took Tate's hand and led her down toward the tracks, up and over them, and straight through the pine needle path toward his house.

"How'd you even do it, Tate?" he asked. "How'd you follow me in the first place. Even that guy—who moved like a doggone ninja—couldn't get over that wall. How did you?"

"Simple," Tate said, dusting her hands with a *clip clap*. "I climbed a tree."

"A tree?"

"There's a pine tree right up close to the outside of the wall," she said. "I shinnied up and climbed far enough onto a branch for it to droop right down over the wall. I only had to jump about six feet. It was easy."

Troy wiped some sweat from his brow and said, "I said it before, Tate, you're like a monkey."

"In a good way, right?" she said.

"Monkeys are cool," Troy said. "You planted the quarter?"

"I gave you the thumbs-up," she said.

"So, how'd you do it?" Troy asked, the glow of his

house appearing through the trees. "You just asked for the bathroom and they all looked away?"

"I just pretended like I was a ditz," she said. "I kept talking. I told them the story about my aunt Mary Ann getting arrested for throwing paint on women walking down Park Avenue."

"What?" Troy said.

"She's with PETA," Tate said. "She's kind of nutty, but I figured, you know, that with all those dead animal skins, at least they'd think I had a point. So I'm telling the story, and I kneel down on that bear rug to explain how my aunt says you can see the pain on the animal's face even after it's stuffed, and I slip that quarter right into his mouth. You think it worked?"

Troy shook his head. "You're crazy. Yeah, I'm sure it worked. But something must have gone wrong. Otherwise, who was that guy?"

"Well," Tate said, hanging her head. "I tried, Troy. I'm sorry if I blew it."

Troy put an arm around her shoulders and gave her a squeeze.

"It's okay, Tate," he said. "Don't worry. I think all this stuff is just going to turn out however it was meant to be. My mom says that all the time and it drives me crazy, but I'm starting to think it's really true. Some things are just meant to be."

"So, what do we do now?" Tate asked.

"My house," Troy said, and they followed the familiar

path to his front door.

When Troy swung the door open, he could tell by the look on his mom's face that something had happened— and it wasn't something good.

CHAPTER SIXTY-FOUR

"TROY, HONEY," **HIS MOM** said, rushing to him and hugging him tight.

"What happened, Mom?" he asked, separating from her.

"You're okay," she said. "That's the important thing."

"Of course I'm okay," he said, nudging Tate so she wouldn't give away the fact that they'd been chased. There was no reason to worry his mom.

"They sent an agent after you, but I guess he didn't catch you," she said.

"Agent?" Troy said, glancing at Tate. She raised her eyebrows and shrugged.

"From the FBI," she said, taking the cell phone back from him and dialing as she spoke. "It happened fast, Troy. They called to tell me. They wanted me to let them know if you got back. The FBI got what they needed on tape right after Tate dropped the quarter. The agents rushed right in, but a couple got away. I guess it was hectic, and they wanted to make sure you and Tate were okay."

"A couple of who?" Troy asked, but his mom was on with an FBI agent, explaining that she had Troy and Tate and that they were fine. Then she hung up.

"Those men," she said, her attention now fully on Troy. "Your father was one of them. G Money had a tunnel the FBI didn't know about. It goes between the main house and a guesthouse behind the pool. From there they got away into the trees. The FBI has a helicopter on its way. Tate must have interrupted their meeting at the perfect time, because the FBI said that the minute she was gone, the men kept right on talking about a money-laundering deal."

"But that's good," Troy said. "I did what they asked me to do, and now they have to help my dad. They got what they want. What's wrong? Why do you look like that, Mom?"

"Well," she said with a pained expression, "it's the money, Troy. The plan was to take it."

"What do you mean?" Troy asked. "What money?"

"The five million dollars from the Jets," she said. "*Your* money. Your father was going to take it, Troy. He was going to give it to those men. He was taking their cash to pay back his investors, then giving them your clean money in return. I'm sorry."

"That can't be," Troy said, the look on his mom's face making him sick because he knew she believed it to be true.

"I blame myself," she said, shaking her head. "People don't change. I know better."

"You can't just take someone's money, Mom," he said, studying her face for the punch line.

"I thought the same thing," she said. "I was going to let him handle it—sign the contract and set up an account for you. I *trusted* him. I'm sorry I have to tell you this, Troy, but I just think you need to know."

Troy's mom took a deep breath. "He told them he would wire your money into an offshore account. That's how they do it, these criminals. It's as fast as pushing the right button on a computer. The FBI can't stop them. Everything happens too fast."

"He wouldn't do that," Troy said, his voice weak and pathetic. "Not to me."

"I'm sorry, Troy," she said, rubbing the back of his head. "He was, but he's going to pay for it now. That wasn't part of the deal."

"But I did this to *help* him," Troy said, glancing back at Tate, who nodded vigorously. "Mom, don't you get it?"

He stared at her, searching.

"I don't want him to go to jail," he said, the word dying on his tongue.

"You're a good boy, Troy," she said, touching his cheek. Then she turned and bolted out of the living room. Troy heard her bedroom door rattle closed, and he turned to Tate.

"Sorry," he said.

Tate shrugged. "It's okay. I understand."

"I wish I did," Troy said.

"She loves you, Troy," Tate said. "A lot. Everything that happened she feels bad about. I think she feels guilty."

"Why?" Troy said, his face screwing up with frustration.

"I think it's a girl thing," Tate said. "It's hard to explain."

Troy grabbed two handfuls of hair and twisted. "I'm going crazy, Tate. This whole thing is a nightmare."

"I'm sorry, Troy," she said in a whisper. "I wish I could help."

Troy let his hands fall to his sides and said, "No one can help."

"Maybe you should call him, Troy," Tate said. "I know this all looks really bad, but maybe there's a reason. I know my mom is pretty extreme with her religion and all that, but she always says God has a reason, and things always work out the way they're supposed to."

Troy looked at her big brown eyes.

"You think my life was supposed to turn into a complete disaster?" he asked quietly. "Famous for something that gets everyone around me acting crazy? My father finally showing up, but it would have been better if he never had? Why would all that happen, Tate?"

Tate shrugged and looked at her feet. Her voice came in a whisper. "I don't know. Maybe it will still be okay. Things happen."

The phone on the kitchen wall rang, and Troy ran to snap it up before his mother could answer from the bedroom.

"Hello?" Troy said.

"Troy? It's me, your dad."

CHAPTER SIXTY-FIVE

TROY COULDN'T SPEAK.

"Are you there?"

"Yes," Troy said in a whisper.

"Did you hear?"

"Yes," Troy said.

"I can explain, Troy," his dad said. "I want to. That's why I ran. I need to see you. I need to tell you. Not the police, not your mom—me. Please, Troy."

"Were you really going to take it?" Troy asked.

There was silence before his father said, "I need to talk to you about that. Can you meet me on your bridge?"

"The FBI are looking for you," Troy said. "There's a helicopter."

"I know," his father said. "But I need to see you first.

265

I never wanted things to be this way. You have to believe me. Will you meet me?"

Troy looked at Tate. She shook her head slowly, no.

"Yes," Troy said. "I'm coming."

He hung up, and his mom appeared in the hallway, asking, "Was that the FBI?"

"No," Troy said, looking directly at her, the words slipping out of his mouth like snakes slithering out of a plastic bucket. "Wrong number."

"I thought you were talking," she said.

"They wanted to know what number they called," he said, the words still slipping past his lips, "and if a Robert lived here. I thought maybe they were looking for Gramps or something."

His mom blinked at him, then said, "Oh. Well, I'm going to lie back down. I've got a migraine coming on, and I want to try to beat it. I'm sorry I just walked out. This whole thing is so . . ."

"It's okay, Mom," Troy said. "I'm okay."

She smiled weakly and put a hand to her forehead. "Good."

When she disappeared, Troy held a finger to his lips and motioned with his head for Tate to follow him outside.

Back through the pines they went, the distant *chop chop* of a helicopter now in the air. When they hit the train tracks, Tate grabbed his arm.

"You think it's safe?" she asked.

Troy took her hand and gently freed it from his arm.

"It's my dad, Tate," he said.

"And others, too, maybe," she said, lowering her voice to a whisper. "I thought you said they were dangerous."

Troy turned on her and said, "Don't worry, Tate. I have to do this alone anyway."

"I'm not saying I won't go with you," Tate said, but he could hear the fear in her voice.

"I need to do this alone," Troy said.

Tate hugged him. He squeezed her tight and felt the bones beneath her skin. He pushed his face into her silky hair, just for a moment, before turning to go.

He didn't look back.

CHAPTER SIXTY-SIX

WHEN TROY REACHED THE edge of the bridge, he could just make out the dark shape of his father in the middle. The *chop chop* of the helicopter seemed closer, but it droned back and forth, still moving without an apparent purpose.

"Dad?" he called out.

"Yes," his father said softly. "It's me, Troy."

Troy stepped out onto the steel bridge, his feet clapping the metal with an empty sound. When he reached his father, he stood facing him, and his dad put a hand on each of Troy's shoulders.

"I know this is where you come to dream your biggest dreams," his father said.

Troy thought he saw the glimmer of tears in his father's eyes. Troy's own eyes began to fill, and he said,

"But this is a nightmare."

"I didn't mean it to be, Son," his dad said, wincing and looking up into the starry sky. "You have to believe that. I was never going to take your money. I was just going to trade it. You have to understand. They said they'd kill me, Troy. I took their money and invested it because I thought I couldn't lose. I was in the big time. It was all going so well—my condo, the planes, the Porsche—and then the economy, it just . . . no one thought it could ever happen. I . . . I . . ."

His father hung his head, and his shoulders sagged. He clasped his hands, wrung them together, and swayed. Over the sound of crickets, Troy heard the growing thump of the helicopter's blades pounding in the night. Above, the fat beam of a spotlight stroked the stars, wavering, and then burst through the trees to light up the bridge. They turned and shielded their eyes against the white light. Troy's father took Troy's arm and pulled him into a tight hug. He squeezed the back of Troy's head so that it almost hurt.

"I'm sorry, Son," his dad said. "I love you, but I have to go."

Behind him, Troy heard the shouts of men.

He opened his eyes. Over his father's shoulder he could see the dark shapes of the agents advancing with flashlights. His father was trapped.

"You can't," Troy said, grasping for a hold on his sleeve even as his father stepped away.

In horror Troy watched as his father ducked beneath a steel beam and turned to face him from the outside edge of the trestle.

"I love you, Troy," his father said, raising his voice above the thundering helicopter. Then his father looked around at the men running toward them and at the helicopter, still beyond the trees but sweeping the branches above with wind from its blades so that they shook and trembled in the swirl of light and noise.

Someone shouted, "Stop!"

Troy's father held up a fist that told Troy to be strong.

Then his father jumped.

The helicopter sprang into the open sky between the trees, its spotlight glaring down at the murky Chattahoochee below.

CHAPTER SIXTY-SEVEN

THEY RODE FOR TEN minutes in Seth's H2 before Troy realized that Nathan wasn't talking to him.

"What's up with that?" Troy asked.

Nathan had his forehead pressed against his window, huffing on the glass and making squeaky designs.

He made a quick star, then said, "Are you really going to abandon us after this game? Sheesh. Some friend."

"Hey," Tate said, "you big meathead. Instead of moping like that, why don't you pump yourself up? So, it's our last game together. Let's not cry about it. Let's win this thing!"

"You wouldn't understand," Nathan said, waving his hand at her. "You're a girl."

"Cut it out, goofball," Tate said. "I mean it. Don't ruin this. Let's go play. Let's have fun. Let's win this."

Seth cleared his throat and said, "Tate's right, Nathan. In football, you never know which game is going to be your last. Look at me."

Troy hung his head.

"No," Seth said to him, messing up his hair, "don't you get down. I didn't mean it like that, Troy. It's just the way it is. You never get to play this game as long as you want. It always ends too soon, and every year, if you are lucky enough to make it, your team changes. Something always changes. That's life. You keep moving."

"Like a shark, right?" Troy said dully, his eyes watching the trees go by.

"What?" Seth said.

"Nothing," Troy said.

"Come on, you three," Seth said. "If nothing else, win this thing for me, will you? I'd like to get a coaching job out of this. Maybe the playing part is over for me, but I'm not leaving this game—not ever, if I can help it."

"Of course we'll win it for you," Tate said. "You made us state champs. You helped Troy, and it looks like he's going to get rich from it. Besides, I want that scholarship money."

Seth laughed at her.

Nathan sighed and said, "I just can't believe this is it for us."

"Who knows, Nathan?" Troy said. "Maybe you and I will play in college together. Georgia Bulldogs?"

Troy turned around and saw Nathan break out into a grin and swipe a hand over his brush cut. "Sheesh, now we're talking."

"And maybe I'll play soccer there," Tate said.

Everyone went silent. Troy looked over the seat at her. She smiled at him.

"But, Tate," he said, "you're a football player—not just a kicker, a real football player. Remember that tackle you made on the kickoff against Dunwoody? You helped win that game."

Tate blushed, looked down at her hands, and said, "I know, but next year it's not junior league anymore; it's the middle school team."

"Some girls play in high school," Troy said. "There's that girl over in Roswell named Bridget Kennicott who's so tough they call her the Tornado."

"But not after that," Tate said. "Even the Tornado won't play in college."

"You could be the first, Tate," Troy said.

"But I could get a full ride as a soccer player," she said, "if I work at it. I'm fast and I'm strong."

"And you got a mean leg," Nathan said.

"And that," she said.

"And tough," Troy said.

"Thank you," Tate said. "So, this really is the last game for us. Let's win it."

Tate held out a hand in the air between them all. Nathan put his hand on top of Tate's, and Troy reached back over the seat to cover them both.

"Win it, on three," Troy said.

"One, two, three, WIN IT!"

CHAPTER SIXTY-EIGHT

TROY AND THE GEORGIA team were down by six and only twenty-seven seconds remained. It was third down and eight yards to go for a fresh set of downs. Troy took the snap from the shotgun position four yards behind the center and read the defense. The team's best receiver—a tall, skinny kid from Valdosta—had the coverage beat, but he slipped on the grass, and Troy immediately looked to his second receiver: the tight end running a post who hadn't been able to get free from the linebacker's jam.

Before Troy could get to his third read, the pocket collapsed around him and his instincts had to take over. Instead of running away from the surge of defenders, Troy stepped up toward them, ducking one, then dodging another, sharply aware of Nathan throwing himself in front of the noseguard to protect Troy's knees. Troy found the seam he was looking for: a narrow opening in the flurry of bodies. In that same instant Rusty Howell broke free down the sideline. Troy took one more step forward, knowing the middle linebacker, on a late blitz, would crack him in the face.

Troy launched the ball and took the shot, seeing stars before he hit the ground. The roar of Georgia fans, clad in red and black, raised him from the ground. His teammates swarmed him, moving as he did toward the goal line, slapping his shoulders, helmet, and back. Tate jogged out and nailed the extra point, then Troy, Tate, and Nathan watched alongside Seth as the Georgia kickoff team kept Florida pinned deep. Their defense stood strong. The clock wound down. The gun went off, and Nathan as well as Tate cackled wildly to Troy about their ten-thousand-dollar scholarship money.

Troy congratulated not just his best friends but the rest of his teammates. Seth gave Troy a hug, then pulled away at the sight of the approaching Georgia Bulldogs' head coach, Mark Richt. The two men shook hands and began to talk. Troy turned and met his mom and Gramps at the fence. They hugged him, too, and said they'd meet him in the tunnel, where only family with passes were allowed to go.

Troy changed into his street clothes and got to the tunnel as fast as he could. He stood waiting with the rest of his teammates, searching the crowd beyond the fence as, one by one, families were allowed into the separate area. In the swarm of arms and legs, banners and pom-poms, hats and grinning faces, Troy spotted a face that made his heart clench. He blinked and looked again.

The face was gone, and Troy had no idea if it had been a dream or not. He staggered toward the fence and gripped the cold metal mesh. Pressing his forehead into the wire, he strained to see it again. For what seemed like a lifetime, he looked. He only stopped when he felt his mom's hand on his shoulder and heard the warm, rough voice of his gramps. Troy stepped away, still looking, still wondering if the smiling, winking face had really been his father's.

ABOUT THE AUTHOR

TIM GREEN, himself an adopted child who has written movingly of his own search for his birth parents in A MAN AND HIS MOTHER, has brought the experience of those feelings to Troy White, whose longing to know his father was evoked in Tim's first novel for young readers, the *New York Times* bestseller FOOTBALL GENIUS. A former star defensive end with the Atlanta Falcons, Tim earned his law degree from Syracuse University and began writing bestselling books for adults and young readers, including THE DARK SIDE OF THE GAME and BASEBALL GREAT. He's worked as an NFL analyst for FOX Sports and most recently hosted *Find My Family* for ABC TV.

Tim lives with his wife, Illyssa, and their five children in upstate New York, where he enjoys sailing and coaching his kids' football and baseball teams. You can visit him at www.timgreenbooks.com.